DUST OF THE *Rabbi*

by Julia Rose

ISBN 979-8-218-15029-7

Cover design by Sam Glorioso

Created in the United States of America

1st printing edition

Dedication

For Jesus.
My Savior, first love, my dear Friend – the One I long to be near all my days

Acknowledgements

I would like to thank my parents, for the ridiculous amounts of hours spent listening to my stories over the years, never failing to show interest and encouraging me to keep writing even when my stories weren't all that good or interesting. Most importantly, thank you for loving Jesus. I watched you walking with the Rabbi as with a dear friend, and it showed me He was truly real, Someone I should approach, too. You were and are my first and most important role models.

I would also like to thank Pastor Sam Glorioso, who pushed me to keep writing this story when I didn't know what came next, confident that God would finish what He started. Our discussions on the story during which the Holy Spirit dropped inspiration were so necessary. Your wisdom, gleaned over time through your mentorship, informs many of the things Yeshua and others say in this book. Hopefully others will grow and learn from it as I have. Also, your work on the cover is beautiful, and your help with the technical intricacies of this book is invaluable. Your partnership makes it much more likely people may pick it up and take this journey with David.

Introduction

This story started out, as most works of literature do, as a single paragraph. Perhaps unlike some other works of literature, it remained as a single paragraph for what must have been over a year, with no intention on my end of it becoming anything more. God, it seems, had other ideas. Over a period of months, I felt a prompting to pick up that one paragraph and try to grow something from it. It was a very gradual impression on my heart, so gradual that I don't really remember how it came to be or how it grew stronger. I do recall that one night, talking with my cousin Isaac on the phone, I said something along the lines of, "You know, I think I'm supposed to do something with that story."

It didn't come easily at first. The first day I took that paragraph and wrote the rest of the scene around it (David meeting Simon in the marketplace), I sat on my bed in my parents' house with tears running down my cheeks, convinced I wasn't cut out for this. "God, this isn't a good idea!" I argued. "I used to write in college, but it's been years. I might have once had the skills but I'm not good enough now. Who am I to do something like this? You've got the wrong person." Then I paused, wiped my face, and figured I'd at least try a bit more…

Looking back at that day, I actually had it backwards. In fact, I would not have been ready to write this story back in my college days. I would have put too much pressure on myself to sound intelligent, and would have been too worried about needing to have themes and subtexts and patterns, references, and layers of complexity. In reality this is a very simple story, and I have learned that simple can be beautiful. John 3:16: "For God so loved the world that He gave His one and only Son, that whoever believes in Him shall not perish but have eternal life." See? Salvation is simple. But oh, isn't it breathtaking?

A few notes before you read on: In this story I call Jesus "Yeshua," which is His Hebrew name and what people would have called Him in His day. The miracles and healings I detail in this story are not pulled from the gospel accounts, but rather they are different things that Jesus might have done, people whose lives He may have touched. Also, I believe that God meant me to write this story and the Holy Spirit led me through the composition of each scene. I believe something in here can be used to reach you, to touch your heart, to enable you to have an encounter with Jesus. So if I may make a request of you, I humbly ask that you read this story with an openness to see where Jesus might want to meet you within it. I hope you use this story as a pair of sandals for you to stand in, in the middle of a dusty road in Israel. A figure of a man approaches in the haze, a very special and different sort of rabbi, and he's headed … straight toward you.

1

A New Old Friend

David was not having the best day. Hitching his satchel higher on his shoulder, he grumbled under his breath as he moved through the market, waving off the merchants like flies who approached him with their goods. His eyes were down as he skirted groups of people with deft movements, his brow creased with displeasure.

These trips to Capernaum always irritated him. He was a lawyer; he had better things to do than cart his mother's handmade wares into neighboring towns to sell for her. It was true that his mother had no one else to go for her; their little village was so small there were few buyers, and at least in a fishing village like Capernaum her homemade nets had some interest. He also had to admit that his own business was slow right now. Still, he always worried that while he was away a potential client would finally come knocking at his door, only to find him gone, and move on to another option.

That was the normal irritant. Another was that this trip so far had gone very poorly. The nets did not sell for nearly as much as he would have liked. He had tried to haggle but the cheap buyer had outdone him, and he felt afterward that the man would have made a rather better lawyer than himself. Such moments of comparison always made him introspective, which made him more irritated. Thus he was, to put it shortly, not in the most agreeable of moods.

"David? David, is that you?"

The loud shout came from behind him. He pretended not to hear, keeping his head down. It was probably some merchant from whom he had mistakenly bought before. They always tried to make themselves one's friends and then make their deals sound special and exclusively marked down as a personal favor.

"David, I know you can hear me! You did that even when we were children!" The burst of hearty laughter that followed made him stop and straighten in surprise. He turned. "Simon?"

The man who shouldered his way through to him, sunburnt face creased in a toothy smile, was most definitely Simon. The big man dropped the baskets he was carrying and swept David up in a bearlike embrace, his hard-muscled arms squeezing him tight with delight. David's arms were trapped against his sides and he felt like his ribs were being crushed. "It's good to see you, Simon," he gasped.

Simon dropped him to his feet again with a slap on the back that made him stumble. "It is wonderful to see you, David. What brings you to Capernaum? I thought you were too busy studying and lawyering to do much mingling with the common folk these days?"

David looked up sharply but Simon was still grinning. He was in a very good mood, it seemed, and the tease was good-natured. David lifted his money pouch. "Selling nets for my mother."

"Ah, yes, she is so industrious, I remember that!" Simon chuckled. He motioned for David to follow and they found an empty merchant stall with a few chairs and sat down out of the sun. "She used to have us out fetching supplies as boys and helping her in whatever crafting she was doing. Always up to something, your mother." He motioned to the baskets at his side. "I was just in town myself to restock on supplies."

David eyed the many loaves of bread and assortment of other food. "You always ate like a bear, Simon, but that's a lot of food even for you. Are you going on a three-month trip into the wilderness?" He paused a moment, uneasy. "You aren't still with that rabbi, are you? Yeshua of Nazareth?"

Simon's smile lessened and his eyes narrowed slightly. "Yes, what of it?"

"You must be joking," David said. "That was months ago that I first heard of you going off with him! You are still on that diversion?"

Simon bristled. "It's not a 'diversion,' David. It's … it's something beyond what I can explain."

David felt his peeved mood returning. "Well you had better try. People have been talking, Simon. Because we were friends as children I have tried to cover for you, saying 'Oh you know Simon, he's always up for a bit of nonsense now and then.' But months? Surely that's a bit excessive."

"It has been more than a year, actually," Simon said evenly.

"*What?*" David exclaimed, clapping a hand to his brow. "You've been off with this teacher for over a year? I had no idea it had been that long. What can you possibly be thinking, Simon?"

Simon's fists clenched on the table. "David," he said in a warning tone.

"Look at yourself!" David cried, gesturing at Simon in exasperation. "You were a successful fisherman who plied a good trade, made a good living. You left your family, Simon, and all your responsibilities, to be a …" He raised his hands. "…a wandering beggar at the feet of a heretical rabbi! What can you possibly say in defense of that?"

Simon's eyes flashed and he stood so quickly he knocked over his chair. "You do not know of what you speak!"

David stood and stepped back, for he knew that look. His old friend was liable to swing out with a fist or a wrathful kick. But to David's astonishment, Simon checked himself. The fire in his eyes died down to a flicker and turned more to frustration than anger.

"I do not know how to explain it," Simon sighed, leaning on the table. "It is not as if I am a wise man or a prophet, to be able to give voice to the changes that have come over my heart since Yeshua invited me to follow him." He frowned and shook his head. "You see, I fail at once. Even the word 'invited' is not right. Yeshua did not invite me to follow him, he commanded it." Seeing David's indignation, Simon groaned and covered his face with his hands. "Yet it was also an invitation – it was both. It was at once a command *and* an invitation."

"How can something be both a command and invitation?" David countered. "The word 'invitation' conveys no accountability or obligation, where 'command' implies imposing one's will directly onto the actions of another."

"Oh do not start that," Simon said. "This is not some legal debate, and I have already said I am no great speaker." He spread his hands. "Just come see him and you will see what I mean. Spend a few minutes listening to him speak, a few minutes in his presence, and you will know why I follow him."

David shook his head. "I don't think so, my friend. Unlike you I have a life I feel obligated to return to. My mother needs her earnings, and my business is missing its proprietor."

"Nonsense," Simon said dismissively, and David frowned. "And first things first," the big man said with a hint of gruffness in his voice. "You should know my family is well looked after by my wife's brother during the times I am away traveling with Yeshua."

David raised his eyebrows but Simon's expression brooked no argument. He kept quiet.

"And as for you, David," Simon continued. "I happen to know your mother very well, and know she wheedled enough money out of you before your trip to be more than comfortable until long after you return, supplemented by her own income cleaning for the rich."

David opened his mouth to protest, though he was unsure what he would say. Simon was right.

"And as much as you whine about being away from your business," Simon said, pressing the attack, "you know you cannot abide sitting all day in your empty office, listening to every movement outside your door hopefully. You told me when last we met that these months in the year are your slowest, more people being away on business, and you do not get much clientele until they return from their journeys weeks from now, complaining to you about the ways they were wronged on their travels."

Simon leaned confidently against one of the stall's posts and crossed his arms, smirking at David, and David snorted in frustration and amusement. Whatever else could be said about Simon, he clearly listened. He knew what David was returning home to and knew David had no valid excuse for not coming to hear Yeshua teach.

He was still about to argue back, but something in Simon's face held him. The other man had become serious again, and his eyes pierced David.

"David, I was looking for something. I did not know what. I was restless – always have been, you know me."

David nodded.

"But I found what I was looking for in listening to Yeshua, in following him. You have to come see him when he speaks, even once, and you will understand. Say you will come."

Simon's tone was sincere and sounded somehow grounded, a different sort of confidence than the bravado David had heard there before. He sounded assured and at rest. The delivery was also gentler than he had expected from Simon. He studied the man's face. Even some of the hardness in the fisherman's weather-beaten features had been softened, and his eyes had a peculiar brightness to them.

He probably just has a fever, David thought with a snicker. Yet as much as he wished to dismiss these incongruities in the Simon he knew and walk away from this request, he found himself hesitating. He could not remember his childhood friend ever committing to anything much besides his marriage and fishing. He certainly did not recall Simon leaning towards the faith of their fathers or having any spiritual inclinations at all. What made him follow this rabbi, this Yeshua, so passionately? And what accounted for these softening changes, what had gentled this beast of a man? David admitted to himself that he was intrigued. He also grudgingly agreed that, despite his anxiety not to miss a client, Simon had been correct: he really was in no hurry to rush back to his empty office.

He sighed. "Fine. I will come see your Yeshua tomorrow, but just to appease my curiosity. Where will I find him?"

Simon's face broke into a broad grin and he clapped David on the arm. "Wonderful!" Then his eyes took on a sly look; he smiled mischievously. "As to where you will find him, just follow the crowds."

"What?" David choked. "You mean you will not take me to him yourself?"

Simon shrugged. "I really cannot say where we will be tomorrow," he commented airily. Then he smirked. "But huge crowds always seem to find Yeshua no matter where he goes. If you see a very large group of people trotting off, join up with them. Just ask them where they are going and why, and you should find a host of traveling companions." He grinned again and picked up his baskets. "I should be getting back to the others." He took a few steps into the street.

"Wait, Simon," David's hand shot out and took hold of Simon's sleeve. "Why can you not take me with you tonight to meet Yeshua yourself?"

Simon frowned. "Ah, what you ask is against his policy. Tonight is one of the evenings when Yeshua has asked just the twelve of us, his closest followers, to stay with him in a private place. He needs these times of quiet to rest."

"Rest?" David laughed. "All he does is talk all day, correct? How much rest can he need?"

A twinkle appeared in Simon's eyes. "Oh, that is not all he does, my friend." He laughed heartily at David's questioning look. "Come find us tomorrow, and you will see for yourself what I mean." He detached himself from David and waved farewell. "Until tomorrow, David. Peace be with you."

"Peace be with you," David muttered in reply with a brief wave. He watched Simon's back receding down the street for a few moments before turning away and making his way back to his inn.

The next morning David woke earlier than he had intended, startled to wakefulness by a crash in the street below his window. Propping himself on an elbow, he listened intently for a few moments, then sighed and flopped onto his back, covering his face with his arm. A collision between the carts of two street vendors, neither of whom had apparently been looking where he was going. He yawned and waited for the argument to die down. It did shortly, blending with the many other cries of street vendors and pleas of beggars until it all became merely the background noise of another Capernaum morning.

David lay on the hard bed, nursing his frustration at being abruptly pulled from slumber. The warmth of the morning sunlight slanting in through the window, however, soon soothed him until he was nearly asleep again. Eyes half open, he lazily turned over in his mind a list of items that should be accomplished that day. There were not many, for which he was grateful. A leisurely day would be a nice change of pace after the last week of business.

Gradually he became aware that the sound from the street outside was growing louder. It was not the sound of another argument or the calls of merchants. He sensed it was mounting excitement. Tuning in, he made out one word being repeated in many different voices: "Yeshua!" He sat up.

"Yeshua!" someone shouted in the street. "Yeshua is coming!"

"Is it really him? I thought he was in Bethsaida!" someone said.

"He has returned, and he is healing many who are sick!"

Healing the sick? David looked toward the window. Are they talking about Simon's Yeshua?

Swinging his legs off the bed, David pushed himself to his feet and shuffled to the window. Leaning out, he watched the happenings in the street below. As word spread that Yeshua of Nazareth had returned, doors opened, heads popped out of windows, and children ran shrieking and laughing out of alleyways and houses, racing toward the edge of town. Women and men began leaving whatever work they were doing and following the children. From his vantage point, David could see a high hillside rising outside the town. That seemed to be where everyone was headed. He thought he could make out the tiny shapes of some people already there.

The news about Yeshua was making its way through the inn as well. He heard voices speaking low in excitement in the hallway and doors opening and slamming, feet rushing down stairs. A young man and woman holding hands exited through the front door below into the street and joined the thickening crowd. David squinted at the sun. Barely the second hour. He sighed and grabbed his clothes. Quickly dressing, he washed his face and hands in a bowl of water, slipped on his sandals, and grabbed his money pouch on the way out.

Stepping out onto the street was rather like wading into a river. By now there were so many people going in one direction that the traffic had its own current. In order to not get bumped into David almost had to join the trek. He tucked his pouch inside his tunic in case of pickpockets and turned into the flow of people. They passed several streets and soon emerged into the main market. Vendors called out for customers, and while they gained one or two by their efforts, most were fixated on getting to that hillside where, from what David understood, Yeshua would be teaching.

Partially because he was hungry and partially because he did not want to appear as eager as everyone else, David decided he would stop for a bite of breakfast before going to see Yeshua. He pushed his way through the throng and walked up to a fruit merchant. He pulled out some coins and asked for some dates.

"There you are," said the merchant sulkily, sliding a packet toward David on the wooden counter. "You know you are only my third sale of the day? By now I should have made at least ten more, but whenever that teacher shows up he steals my customers away."

"Have you ever gone to see him yourself?" David asked.

"What? And lose more of the day by being away from my stand? No." The man glanced toward the hillside and hesitated. Then he shook his head. "No." He grabbed a broom and started busily sweeping the ground in front of his stand.

By the time David made it to the base of the hill, there was hardly any place left to sit. So many had come to see this strange rabbi. David looked around at the faces of those who had come to listen and felt himself to be separate from them. He almost pitied them. They seemed so full of expectation and hope, but why? They wanted to hear something good, and because everyone else said this fellow had something good to say, well then he must be worth seeing. It was something David deeply disliked. He almost felt wrong to be among them, lest anyone think he was one of them. He shook his head and kept climbing the hill, searching for a good seat. He could have sat at the base of the hill but he had decided he would only come to hear Yeshua once, make his dismissal, and let Simon know just how mad he thought he was and let it be done. So he needed to have a decent view.

Finally he found a free patch of grass, next to the young couple from the inn. They smiled at him as he squeezed in next to them. He dipped his head briefly before turning his attention to the man who was speaking.

At first he had difficulty locating him. He heard the voice but could not identify the speaker. No one looked particularly more likely to be Yeshua than another. Then he saw him. A man dressed in fine clothes and sitting erect with the air of a statesman. Odd, though, that the words kept coming but his mouth wasn't moving. But surely… Wait, there he was! David cocked his head to one side. What was this? The man who was speaking was sitting with the children, hunched over, with one of them on his back, hanging off him like a monkey. He was smiling and tickling the child as he talked, and the little boy laughed and squirmed. Surely this could not be Yeshua.

David began listening to his words. "And so I say to you, if anyone gives even a cup of cold water to one of these little ones who is my disciple, truly I tell you, that person certainly will not lose his reward." He patted the child on the back and had him sit down next to him. "Children, would you like to hear a story?"

"Yes, teacher, yes!" the children shouted. "Tell us a story!"

"Very well," he chuckled. He looked up at the adults. "This story will be told in a way the children will understand and enjoy, but pay attention, because this story is for everyone." He winked. "Even adults." Hunching over, he got eye-level with the children. "Some of you may already know this story," he said, "because I think I told it last time I was here. I want to tell you why it is so important that you listen to what I say to you." He sat up straight and folded his hands. "Now, I will need a few volunteers to help me tell this story." A broad smile lit his face as every child's hand shot eagerly into the air. 'All right... Matthias! Yes, you can be a part of this. And..." Leaning back, Yeshua surveyed the crowd. For a moment David thought their eyes met and he started and glanced away. A moment later, "--Peter, I'll need your help for this!" He motioned, and a man stood up in the crowd and picked his way over people to stand at Yeshua's side. It was Simon. David tilted his head, confused. *Peter? Why is he calling Simon 'Peter'?*

Yeshua stood and positioned the child he had chosen next to Simon. "Matthias, you will be playing the role of the wise man."

The little boy beamed and stood on his tiptoes.

"Peter, you will be the foolish man. Shouldn't be too hard for you, eh?" The crowd laughed, as did Simon. Yeshua clapped him on the back playfully. "Now, let us begin." He turned toward the crowd. "Whoever hears what I say to you and puts my words into practice is like a wise man who built his house on the rock." He looked down at the boy Matthias, who was grinning out at the audience. He nudged the boy. "Build your house, build your house!" he whispered loudly. Matthias jumped and began gesturing as if he were hammering, measuring, and raising up a house. He stamped his foot on the ground as if to say that the foundation was solid, looking quite pleased with himself.

While he was doing this, Yeshua had picked a few more children for the story. "And the rain fell, and the floods came, and the winds blew and beat on that house--" He pointed to them, and they surrounded Matthias, waving their arms and stomping their feet, making sounds like whooshing wind and crashing waves. "—But the house did not fall, because it had been founded on the rock." Matthias did a good job looking entirely unconcerned at the "wind" and "water" all around him. He even faked a yawn.

"But!" Yeshua said, raising his hand high and pointing a finger. "Everyone who hears my words and does not put them into practice will be like a foolish man," he said, pointing to Simon, who wore a comical expression on his face, "who built his house on sand." Simon too began miming as if he were building a house, but he kept losing his footing in the shifting sand that was supposedly under his feet. Yeshua got the attention of the children who were still surrounding Matthias and pointed dramatically at Simon. "And the rain fell and the floods came, and the winds blew and beat against that house, and it fell, with a great crash!" With that, the children charged Simon and he let them knock him over, giggling and climbing on him.

David looked around him as Yeshua had his players take a bow. Generally, the people seated near him were smiling and seemed pleased with the lesson. There were some, though, who looked on with narrowed eyes. A few looked irritated. For himself, David did not like it at all. Yeshua had just made a ridiculous claim about the importance of his own teachings, and hardly anyone seemed bothered by it. He cleared his throat. "Excuse me, sir," he said loudly.

"Yes?" Yeshua, still smiling, glanced around until he spotted David. Simon saw him and grinned, obviously surprised to see him there.

"You make a bold claim, teacher." David hid a smile as Simon's expression darkened. "You say," he continued, "that people who follow your teachings are to be considered wise and will have no troubles, as if you have some particular wisdom beyond that of others. You also say that those who do not follow your teachings are not only to be considered foolish, but that they should expect calamity to fall upon them!" He crossed his arms. "It seems you think rather much of yourself."

Murmurs rose in the crowd; people shifted uncomfortably. David could see several of those who had seemed irritated nodding in agreement.

"I appreciate your willingness to speak out, friend," Yeshua said calmly, still smiling slightly. "All I can say is that I speak the truth. My words are sound, and those who follow what I teach are indeed wise, though not in the way this world would recognize. Also," he said, lifting a finger. "You misquote me. Both the wise man and the foolish man experienced trials – the elements assailed both houses. All experience tribulation in life; there are no exceptions. The difference in the outcome of the storm in the story was dependent upon the foundation, and the same is true when we experience pain, suffering, and struggles in life. What you build your life upon determines whether you will stand or fall when the storm comes upon you."

"And people should build their lives upon your words?" David pressed.

Yeshua nodded. "Yes." He raised his hands as David opened his mouth to argue. "I want to point out that what I say is what is at the heart of the law. For I did not come to abolish the law, but to fulfill it." He dipped his head genially and turned his attention back to the crowd. "Let me tell you another story…"

As much as David wanted to respond, he was not certain how to process Yeshua's last statement about fulfilling the law. And Yeshua's comments were rather compelling. There was a strange certainty, mixed with what seemed to be humility, in his reply that David found at once off-putting and appealing. He glanced about; the crowd was already engrossed in the teacher's next story. Settling back in the grass, he decided he might as well listen for a while longer.

2

A Welcome Invitation

What must have been several hours later, Yeshua stood up and dismissed the crowd. Apparently the teaching was over for the day. As he stood up and stretched with everyone else, David noticed that he felt disappointed. When he saw that Yeshua gathered a smaller group of men about him and began drawing away over the hill, he felt a twinge of dismay.

Simon was among them, and was looking at him. He waved and crossed quickly to David. "So, you made it!" He grinned and slapped David on the arm. "What did you think?"

"Interesting, to be sure," David replied, rubbing a smudge of dirt on his tunic casually. "You did not seem pleased when I questioned him, though."

Simon grunted. "I most certainly was not. At first I wanted to hit you. But then I reasoned you are, well, *you*, and it is your way to be contentious."

David shrugged.

Someone from Yeshua's group called for Simon. He turned and acknowledged them. "I have to go, but I will see you again soon."

David suppressed a sigh and shrugged again. "All right."

His friend half-turned away, then swung back. "You would not be interested in coming with us, would you? We are going to eat supper at a friend's house this evening, and I am sure you would be welcome."

"Ah, well…" David said, hoping to hide his eagerness, "I suppose I could come along." He smirked. "Your friend Yeshua is unusual; I would like to observe him further. Also, I have nothing better to do."

"Well then!" Simon exclaimed, putting an arm around David's shoulders. "You shall have opportunity to observe him up close during supper." He led David to join the others of Yeshua's group. As they walked, David glanced back at the dispersing crowd, hoping no one would see him going off with this strange band.

"Yeshua!" Simon said, and David realized he was being pulled toward the front of the group.

"Simon, don't!" he whispered. He wanted to watch from the edges, not be introduced in front of this man's closest followers. Several men noticed him for the first time and shot him annoyed glances. They remembered him from earlier when he questioned their leader. He had a feeling he would not be the most popular dinner guest that evening.

Yeshua turned, his arm slung around the shoulder of a young man. They had been laughing. The youth's smile lessened when he saw David, and he glanced at Yeshua uncertainly. David could see the teacher recognized him, but his smile stayed broad. David did not detect any ill will in Yeshua's expression.

"Yeshua," Simon said as they reached him. "This is my friend David. He would like to join us for our evening meal."

"Ah yes, my debate partner," Yeshua said, crossing his arms. "So you've come to see how things are in the enemy's camp, eh?"

David began to bristle until he saw the twinkle in Yeshua's eyes and realized he was joking.

"Not at all," David said, eyeing those around Yeshua who did not seem to share their teacher's lightheartedness. "Your words intrigued me, teacher. So …" It was at this moment, mid-sentence, that David realized he had not yet determined why he felt the need to linger around Yeshua. He paused. "So..." He groped for words that weren't coming. He felt his ears burning with embarrassment.

"Certainly. You are most welcome to dine with us, friend," Yeshua said, and David silently exhaled in relief. "We are going to the house of a dear friend who I know will not mind one more at the table. We are glad to have you." He motioned to his followers, and the group continued walking. Two men pushed past David and joined Yeshua at the front. Judging by their rigid gestures and the looks they shot his way, he could tell they were angry that he was being brought along.

Simon growled. "I wish James and John would stay out of things. It is none of their concern."

"Ehh, the master will set them right," said a voice on David's other side. "Just watch, the Sons of Thunder will be peaceable after he talks with them."

David turned and saw someone he did not expect. "Andrew?"

The man grinned and the two embraced. "It is good to see you again, David!"

David pulled back and put a hand on Andrew's shoulder. "I had heard the rumors that you went with Simon on this insane trip, but I personally thought between the two of you that you were the wiser brother. I assumed you were too level-headed to be swept up in something like this."

Andrew exchanged a humorous glance with Simon. "You supposed wrong." He laughed. "I was actually the first to decide to follow Yeshua; I came and told Peter."

"Peter?" David asked. "Yes, what is the purpose of that? I heard Yeshua call Simon 'Peter' earlier."

Simon's eyes grew thoughtful. "It is a name Yeshua calls me. The others have started to pick it up as well."

"Why is that?"

"It happened when--" Andrew said, but Simon shot him a warning glance. "Ah, well, Yeshua is an interesting man. Very interesting. You will see as you get to know him."

David raised his eyebrows. "All right, that was strange, but I will not press the matter. And I highly doubt I will stay long enough to get to know Yeshua. That does not interest me; I am just here for a good meal and a bit more observation." He pointed toward the front of the group. "That young man laughing with Yeshua, who is he?"

Andrew smiled. "That is Ari. He is like a little brother to all of us. Yeshua called him to follow him a while ago and they have been inseparable ever since."

"Ari is timid," Simon said. "I wish he would speak up more. He has good things to say."

Andrew chuckled. "Peter, compared to you, everyone is timid!"

They laughed, and David felt his defenses lowering. As the brothers continued talking, he found himself half listening; he tuned in to the hushed voices and bursts of laughter coming from others in the group. The tension of his introduction had eased. He noticed that one of the two men who had accosted Yeshua looked at him with annoyance, but his fellow, who had evidently calmed, looked at David with an apologetically friendly air. No one else seemed perturbed, and he let himself relax.

As he walked, with people behind and in front of him, he appreciated that he was not walking alone. Perhaps it was because he was outside an unfamiliar town and evening was approaching, but the friendly banter and conversations surrounding him seemed rather more welcoming than a solitary trek. In fact, if he allowed himself for the moment to forget that they were following a strange rabbi possessed of some radical notions, he could almost imagine that this was a pleasant, normal group of friends. Not that they were his friends, or that he even had much experience with friends and moments like this, having long been solitary. But he could not say, strolling along now, that he disliked the company.

After walking for a while longer, during which time the light waned in the late afternoon sky until it was truly evening, they arrived at a small house. As soon as they were within eyesight, a man came running out the door and flung himself at the feet of Yeshua. David recoiled, but Yeshua laughed and took the man's hands, raising him to his feet. The man embraced him and then led him inside, chatting animatedly. Yeshua grinned at everyone behind him and beckoned them to follow. Inside, the man and his wife had prepared a meal for them all. As everyone spread out around the table, David noticed that there were several women in Yeshua's group. He reached over to Andrew. "Andrew," he whispered. "Why are there women with you? Are they the wives of some of the men?"

Andrew shook his head. "No, they have chosen to follow Yeshua independently. He allows both men and women to follow him in his travels. It was strange for us too at first, but we got used to it. They are like sisters to us now."

David frowned as he dipped his bread in oil. "These women are like sisters, and Ari is like a little brother. Do all who follow Yeshua come to hold such dear positions?"

Andrew shrugged, sipping his drink. "We're a family. When Yeshua called us to follow him he said we would become fishers of men. I still do not fully grasp what he meant, though I think I am beginning to. We share his message, casting it out like a man casts a net. Those who listen are like fish. But when they start to follow Yeshua they become part of this growing family."

"From fish to family," David chuckled. "An odd notion, wouldn't you say?"

"Odd with the analogy, yes, but I find it beautiful," Andrew said with an earnestness that caught David's attention. "You know that Peter and I have been on our own for years. Peter got married but I never did. When I left my nets to follow Yeshua I did not know I was gaining a family. I am very grateful to him for that."

David let a moment pass, fiddling with a crumb of bread on the table. "I appreciate what you say, Andrew, and I am glad you feel close to these people, but… I would just caution you to be careful. Yeshua may seem like he cares, and this may appear a great and wondrous cause you have joined, but please be wise. I do not want to see you hurt."

Andrew smiled. "And I appreciate your concern, David. Do not take my word for it – watch and see for yourself. You say you want to observe, and I gladly encourage you to do so." He pointed. "Now, could you please pass me some more bread?"

David did so, and the talk fell to other things. David had forgotten how much he liked Andrew. The man was like Simon in some ways but was much calmer, more reserved. Andrew was more of a thinker than his brother, a trait that David valued. He found in Andrew someone he could discuss ideas with, and he realized he was thirsty for such company. They had a very enjoyable conversation as they ate. The meal provided was simple but hearty, and David enjoyed every bite – particularly, he admitted to himself, because he was not paying for it.

Midway through the meal, Yeshua cleared his throat and said, "Now, let's hear from someone. Ari, why don't you tell us a parable?"

A few seats down the table the young man froze, a bite of vegetables lifted halfway to his mouth. "A parable, Yeshua?" He glanced around nervously at the faces watching him. "Are you certain?" He looked around again and lowered his voice. "*Now?*"

The teacher's eyes gleamed. "Yes, now." He leaned toward Ari, smiling, and whispered back. "I want you to practice."

Ari reluctantly put down his food and wiped his hands. "Well..."

"You can use one of mine," Yeshua said. "How about one of the ones from today?"

"Yes, all right." Ari cleared his throat and took a deep breath. "The kingdom of heaven is like treasure hidden in a field. A man found it one day, then hid it again. He went, full of joy, and sold all that he had and bought the field." He picked up his food and continued eating.

Yeshua burst out laughing and slapped the table. "But that was the shortest one!"

Ari smiled. "I was nervous." His eyes glinted with mischief. "And you only said 'a parable' – you did not specify the length!"

Everyone at the table laughed. "All right," Yeshua said, leaning forward and shooting the others a comical glance. "Let me be more specific!" He rested his chin on a fist, considering Ari through half-closed eyes. "The parable of the sower." He held up a hand when Ari opened his mouth to speak. "And explain what it means afterward."

Ari's eyes widened. Yeshua gave him an encouraging nod, and to his credit the youth took a breath, steadied himself, and went into the narrative at an easy, conversational pace. He described a man who sowed seed in his field, but the seed fell in several different areas. None but the seed sown on good soil survived to produce a harvest. The seed in that good soil, however, produced a wonderful crop, much more than was sown. Ari went on to explain that it was another parable about the "kingdom of heaven," though David was not sure to what that referred. He could tell that Ari was a little flustered when explaining the meaning, probably his nerves showing.

When Ari had ended, everyone applauded. Yeshua nodded at Ari with a look of pride and approval. David saw the young man sit straighter, his eyes shining.

The talk of sowing seed reminded David of Andrew's description of casting nets as "fishers of men." He felt uncomfortable, wondering in which category of soil they would classify him, and grew even more uncomfortable as he wondered if he was a fish they were trying to catch. Despite his discomfort, however, he assured himself that all was well. He was just observing. And David surprised himself that he did not feel as put off as he might have expected. Instead, for good or ill, he felt curious to learn more.

After a while the meal eventually wound down. Yeshua was the first to stand, and the others took their cue from him. As they were thanking the host and making their way toward the door, David edged around to the man who had hosted them. "My thanks for letting me join you tonight," he said.

The man was beaming. "Any friend of Yeshua's is always welcome in my home," he said.

"How do you know Yeshua?"

The man looked surprised. "Oh, I thought you knew!" His face creased into the look of a man who was about to share a delicious secret. "You see that over there?" he said, pointing to a rolled-up mat in a corner of the room.

"Yes."

"That was mine. You see…" He wriggled with glee. "I was a paralytic."

David stared at him. "A paralytic?"

The man laughed and clapped his hands. "Unbelievable, isn't it? I mean--" He jumped up and clicked his heels together. "You would never believe it seeing me now, would you? And yet it is true. For years and years I lay on that mat at the side of the street, and my friends begged for money on my behalf. I could not take care of myself, and more to my pain, I could not marry the woman I loved – I could not provide for her. And then one day Yeshua walked by. But unlike so many, He saw me. He really saw me. He saw my need, came to my aid, and healed me with a word. Can you imagine it?" He laughed again.

David frowned. "I'm having some difficulty."

The man missed his skeptical comment, having turned to say goodbye to others who were filing past. He turned back to David and put his hands on his shoulders. "All because of Yeshua. I can hardly believe it myself some days. But I can provide for myself now, and for my wife, who waited for me and who I have now married. And now we are expecting a child. We can afford to bring life into this world, and my family name will not die with me."

His smile was so genuine and infectious that David could not help but smile back. It was clear at least that this man believed his own story. As he bid him farewell and walked out of the house, he felt concerned that he did not feel more concerned. That was a ridiculous claim, that Yeshua had healed a paralytic. But medicine had come farther than he probably was aware. Maybe Yeshua had even just been near when the man's body righted itself on its own. Who knew?

But as David followed along with Yeshua's disciples, he thought how that joy the man expressed seemed connected to the joy Yeshua exuded, the joy Andrew shared. It all seemed to fit together somehow, like a mosaic with a design mysteriously beautiful and compelling. He shook his head.

"David," Yeshua called. He dropped back from the front of the group and fell in step beside David. "Would you like to stay with us tonight? We have no rooms but will spend tonight around a fire under the heavens – so there is plenty of room!" He smiled.

"Yes," David heard himself saying. "I would very much like that, Yeshua."

Yeshua placed a hand on David's shoulder. "Good. And I want you to know, from me, that you are welcome to stay with us as long as you like." He squeezed his shoulder warmly, then made his way over to Ari. David could hear him encouraging the youth on a job well done telling the parable, and they started discussing how Ari could do even better sharing in the future.

At a certain point along the road Yeshua indicated they were leaving the path. The women and a few men, Ari included, bid goodnight to Yeshua and continued down the road into town. David felt unsure for a moment and wondered if he had misheard Yeshua, if he should leave with them. He felt Yeshua's eyes on him and saw him beckon him to follow with the remaining twelve men. For a moment David's reservations about this man came to mind. Then he heard Andrew's laughter at some joke being shared, and remembered that inexplicable, compelling joy. David glanced at the sky, and decided to let himself deal with working out all his questions tomorrow. For now, he would just follow.

They soon found a place to sleep. A fire was started, and they gathered around its warmth. Yeshua talked a little at first, but a man named Bartholomew fell asleep sitting up and almost fell over before waking with a snort, and everyone howled with laughter. Much playful joking followed, and they started telling funny stories about each other. David looked over at Yeshua to see if he was displeased his teaching had been derailed; Yeshua was shaking with laughter. At this something loosened in David and he felt comfortable joining in. He laughed along as story after story was shared. He even ended up sharing a story of his own, highlighting a hilarious misadventure from his, Simon, and Andrew's childhood. It felt so good to laugh deeply and about things purely funny with no irony or satire. When at long last they lay down to sleep, David's heart felt swollen with goodness, and he did not question it. He fell asleep smiling.

3

Attitude of the Heart

The next morning, David woke gradually. He became dimly aware of talking and of movement around him, but he felt so comfortable and safe that he did not bother opening his eyes. He drifted in and out until a hand shook him gently. He opened his eyes.

It was Yeshua. The teacher was kneeling next to him and had a smile on his face. "Good morning!" he said cheerfully. "We let you sleep as long as we could, but we figured you probably would not want to miss breakfast." Beyond Yeshua, the fire had been relit and the men were warming bread over the flames and passing around raisin cakes and figs. Yeshua smiled again and stood, returning to the men huddled around the fire. He crossed his arms. "Well then. I get up for one moment and already Ari has taken my seat. I see you thought you'd join us for breakfast."

Ari grinned up at him. "I just made it here from town – you know how we youngsters are, we never pass up a free meal."

Yeshua groaned. "Oh, I know. Our purse is lighter for knowing you. You always eat like you've just survived a seven-year famine." He ruffled Ari's hair and chuckled. "Nonetheless, I'm glad you're here." He glanced around the tightly packed circle for a few moments, then spread his hands in exasperation. "So no one is going to make room for me?" The disciples laughed and James and Philip scooted apart. Yeshua sat down hurriedly between them, jokingly elbowing them for more room.

David rolled onto his back, closed his eyes, and breathed deeply. He inhaled the scent of the fire and the food, and he listened to the laughter around the breakfast circle. He wanted to savor this moment.

"David, get over here!" Simon yelled at him. "The food's nearly gone." He let out a sizeable belch.

"I wonder how that happened," commented Andrew drily.

And there went the moment. David sighed and rolled over, shaking his head and smiling. He got up and approached the circle, wondering if he would have to jostle his way in to get food. But Ari and Simon, who were seated next to each other, made room for him immediately. As he sat he heard Yeshua laugh and say, "At least someone is shown respect around here."

Breakfast was wholesome but quick, and they were soon walking. Crowds, larger than the day before, soon found them, and Yeshua went up on another hillside to teach them. Although he had enjoyed his time with the group, David still felt uncomfortable with the idea of being associated with Yeshua, so he sat further away down the hillside this time. This choice did not serve him well, however, for a short time later he had a poor vantage point when Yeshua apparently healed a man with a deformed hand. All David saw, from a distance, was a man holding out his arm, Yeshua touching him, and then gasps and shouts from the crowd. He did not know what he was watching until the report was passed back from person to person. There were many cries of "Praise God!" and "Hosanna!" as the crowd's volume swelled and people rose to their feet in excitement. Eventually order was restored and everyone was made to sit down again.

"It's a trick, that's all." said a man a few people to David's left. He looked around. "How do we really know the hand was crippled? He could have just been holding it funny."

"I believe Yeshua has that power," said a woman in front of David. "I have seen him do a miracle before. That time it was with water. He turned it into wine."

The man beside her nodded. "It's true, I was there, I saw it happen. We were serving at a wedding, and the host ran out of wine. Yeshua told us to keep filling jars with water. As we did it, as sure as we're sitting here, the water turned into wine!" He grinned. "Really good wine, too – the best I ever tasted."

The first man rolled his eyes and said, "You're touched in the head. That can't happen, any more than a crippled hand can be made whole. It's impossible."

They shrugged, unbothered by him, and stood up. "Are you ready?" the man asked the woman.

She laughed. "I suppose. We came all this way to see him, but now I'm almost nervous enough to stay here."

The man took her hand. "Come on."

"Do you think he'll remember us?" the woman asked as they moved away.

"Lost cause, the both of them. Believing in things like that," the heckler sneered. "Beyond me how they let themselves get taken in."

"Then why are you here?" someone nearby demanded.

The man wrinkled his nose. "Just wanted to see what all the commotion was about." He got unsteadily to his feet. "But I've seen enough. What you say is impossible. You'd better leave too, before you get pulled in by this charmer." As he walked away down the hill, David noticed he walked with a limp, and looked down to see he had a twisted foot. He glanced back up the hill, saw the man who claimed healing holding his hand up and laughing, and glanced back at the heckler, who was struggling to make it down the hill. He got up and followed the man, and offered his arm for the final steep section.

As they walked, David asked, "I am curious, why would you not take a chance and ask Yeshua to help you? What if he could heal you?"

The man groaned. "You are not one of his followers too, are you? I had you pegged as a wiser man from what you said when he taught yesterday. Caught you in his net already, has he?"

The words reminded David of his conversation with Andrew the day before. *A fish in a net.* He blushed. "No! I'm not, I was just saying 'What if.' "

"Uh huh, of course. Well I'm not such a fool, that's why. False hope is all it is, and I'm not for it."

When they reached the base of the hill the man thanked him gruffly. "I can take it from here."

David watched as he hobbled away and wondered what to do now. Was the man right? Surely Yeshua could not *heal.* That was such a ridiculous and dangerous notion, and it was the second time it had come up, the first being their host the previous day. He should really follow this man's example and walk away too.

But as he watched the man, limping painfully and dragging his lame foot along the ground, David thought further. It wasn't just the man's foot that was twisted. His heart seemed twisted, too, bent around bitterness, like he had closed himself off to hope of any kind. David did not want to be like that. And, wincing, he admitted to himself that he had had a very similar tone when he called out and argued with Yeshua the previous day. That probably should change.

David also remembered the joy and conviction of their host. He had been so sure Yeshua had healed him, and his life had changed dramatically since then. Very well, it warranted further logical thought. Purely for the sake of argument: What if Yeshua *could* heal? David glanced at the limping figure moving away down the road. If it was true, then this man had just missed the opportunity of a lifetime. David resolved that he would not be so hasty. Why not just listen and observe more? Listening could not harm him. He was not a fish caught in the net, he was just taking everything in. In a way, he himself was the fisherman, gathering information in his own net. He would sort through what he gathered and toss away whatever did not make sense, whatever did not suit him. Feeling more secure in his position, and eager to not miss any more of Yeshua's teaching, David turned and went back up the hill.

After a shorter time than David expected, Yeshua dismissed the crowd and gathered his followers to him. David saw Simon wave him over. He was glad to be included in the smaller group again, and smiled at Yeshua when he welcomed him back.

Walking for a bit, they found a spot to rest, and they spread out on the ground, lounging under the shade of several trees. They ate from the food supply and argued about who would be sent into the next town on their travels to resupply. Then several of the disciples started playing a game, for which David joined them, while others sat idly chatting.

Throughout the afternoon David noticed that Yeshua paid particular attention to Ari, going out of his way to sit next to him for the game, and then talking with him afterward. It was evident how much the two enjoyed each other's company. At several points during the game they made each other laugh so hard that tears streamed down their faces. And later, in moments when he glanced over from the conversation he was having with Andrew, Simon, and Philip, David saw them in deep discussion. Theirs seemed a very solid friendship. He thought that Yeshua every now and then looked sad, but those moments were so fleeting that he could never be sure it had really been sadness in the teacher's face.

It was just after the sun had begun to set, and people were beginning to discuss making their way to the house of their friend who was hosting them for the evening meal. David stood and stretched, and began making himself ready to travel. With a start, he realized he did not have his money pouch. He searched through his satchel and asked the others if they had seen it, and soon it became evident he had left it at their last resting spot. He groaned, certain someone had probably found it and taken it. After being assured they would wait for him, David headed back the way they had come.

It took him longer to find the spot than he had anticipated and he searched feverishly for several minutes before locating it and trotting hastily down the road to join the others.

When he drew near to the place, he saw in the dwindling light that everyone was gathered around Ari, laughing and patting him on the back and hugging him. Then the main group started heading down the road toward their dinner host's house. Yeshua stayed back with Ari and talked with him in low earnest tones. David hung back, purposefully far enough away from the two men to not overhear what was being said, but close enough to observe them. He did not know what was going on, but he felt it was important and was interested to watch and see what would happen. Then, to his chagrin, Yeshua turned in his direction and waved him over.

As he approached, Ari nodded one final time, sniffed, and hugged Yeshua tightly. Then he stepped back, dried his eyes, and smiled at Yeshua with a strange confidence and peace. He nodded at David. "Goodbye, friend." He looked at Yeshua. "Until we meet again." He turned from them and began walking down a path David had not noticed before, which led away from the clearing in a different direction from the way they came and the way they were going. He glanced back once, and Yeshua raised a hand to him. He smiled, and did not look back again.

They watched him in silence for some time until he started to shrink into the distance. Finally David said, "Do you mind if I ask what just happened?"

There was a pause, then Yeshua sighed. "I sent him out."

So this is why he had been so much with Ari today. He was enjoying one last day together. This had been his plan. But why? David thought of how much Ari and Yeshua enjoyed each other, how Yeshua mentored him and cared for him. It seemed wrong that he had sent Ari away. For what purpose could that be? "Teacher," said David, glancing between the shrinking form and Yeshua. "You love him like a brother. I've seen the joy he brings you. Why would you send him away?"

Yeshua's eyes never left the young man's diminishing silhouette; David thought he could see moisture shining in the teacher's eyes. "My love for Ari is indeed great. But if I keep him with me here, he will not become who I know he is meant to be. It is better for him to go out into the world, taking what he has learned with me and sharing with others. As he does, his love for me will deepen, as he reflects on our time together and speaks my words to others. My prayers will cover him, and my own love for him will remain strong. Being out there, Ari will grow into a lion. When we meet again--" he chuckled, wiping away a tear with his thumb. "How I already long for the day – When we meet again, we will meet as closer than when we parted, and I will see with my own eyes the Ari I always knew he could be, more complete and fully realized than the day he left." His eyes flicked to David, a slight smile playing on his face. "Do you see? It is for Ari's own good. I am so proud of him, and so excited to see all he will grow to be and all he will do. I just want to see him become who he is meant to be."

David swallowed. The look in Yeshua's eyes was one of such deep, abiding love that it overwhelmed him. He looked away and nodded.

Yeshua sighed and picked up his cloak from the ground. "Come, friend. It is time for supper."

The walk to the house was quiet, with neither man saying anything. David was mulling over what he had witnessed. He had doubted that Yeshua truly loved those who followed him, but that skepticism was washed away. He knew now. How could he not know, after what just happened? The heart of the man keeping pace next to him was so large, so giving. Yeshua, whatever else may be, cared deeply for those who attached themselves to him. They arrived at the house and the meal commenced with Yeshua's appearance as the guest of honor. During the meal, David's eyes frequently wandered to Yeshua's area of the table, and whenever he met the teacher's eyes, he saw that same deep love, and he also felt a sense of connection, because he had been with Yeshua when Ari left. He knew the emotion and state of the teacher. The eyes of Yeshua seemed to thank him for having shared that moment, for asking and for truly listening.

The next day as the group traveled, David's mind worked over a new development: He was not certain what to make of this sudden tie between himself and Yeshua, but he could not deny that he now cared for the man. The love Yeshua displayed so freely made him somehow beautiful, like a sunrise is beautiful, a distant magnificence that still has warmth that can be felt. David thought he might be able to see now why Simon talked about him the way he did. Reverence, awe, he understood a bit more today.

Over the next few days he felt something else growing, too: Confusion. He listened to Yeshua's parables when he taught the crowds, he heard the way Yeshua spoke about the Lord, about Yahweh. There seemed to be a depth of understanding and wisdom that simply could not be accounted for by his rough country upbringing. He was a Nazarene after all, and what good ever came from Nazareth? And yet here he was, teaching thousands of people day in and day out, things that made more sense than David had ever heard, and yet seemed more elusive to truly grasp. And the authority with which he spoke! No rabbi or scholar under whom David had ever studied sounded half as authoritative as Yeshua. That is not to say they did not sound knowledgeable or confident or even pompous, fed by their own egos. Yeshua did not sound pompous; he had no need. When he spoke, it simply sounded as though he knew what he was saying was absolute truth, and that he was the one given the authority to make it known. More than that: it sounded like he had intimate knowledge of all the things of which he spoke, as if he were the very author of truth, and was pleased to make it known to those for whom he had prepared it. David marveled at the man. His confidence seemed unshakable and his wisdom limitless.

His kindness, too, was unending. Most of the time Yeshua was being nearly overrun by crowds of people pushing to be near him. Sometimes it was all the disciples could do to keep people from crushing each other in their desperation to reach him. And yet with this constant demand for his time and the neediness of those asking for it, Yeshua never became cross. It wasn't because he was not tired. David could see the weariness in his face at times. There were moments – when they were just sitting down to eat after a long dusty day of walking or had finally broken away from the throngs of people for a moment of peace – when someone would appear with their sick child or a blind man would call from the roadside. Yeshua made time for them all, and he always did it with compassion. David could not understand it.

Yeshua did disappear at times, and Simon told him he went away to be alone with God, who Yeshua called his father. It must be nice, David thought, to feel so close to the Lord to call him one's father. Yeshua always came back from those times looking brighter and refreshed. Yeshua also often carved out periods of time where it was just him and his disciples – and David. David was not sure why Yeshua let him stay with them in those moments, but he was glad. Yeshua would teach them and answer questions, and these would also be times to rest, have fun together, and relax.

It was during one of the quiet moments that Yeshua and his disciples had together, sitting and enjoying each other's company, when the demon-possessed man attacked.

4

A Song That Heals

They were in the hills and away from the crowds, secreted in a little valley with soft grass and a burbling stream. They had just finished a meal; some were sitting while others took the opportunity to lie down. David was among those who had decided to stretch out on the grass. The sun warmed his face and stomach deliciously, and the heat soaked into his sore feet and calves. It felt so good to not be on his feet. Around him he could hear the muted tones of several conversations. David's attention flitted lazily between them; he was happy to simply be still and rest. He turned his face to the side, resting his head on his arm. The brightness in the sky lit each blade of grass and tiny flower with brilliant color to the point that it overwhelmed him. He closed his eyes, listening to the drone of nearby insects mingling with the sound of the stream. He sank deeper into the peace of the afternoon.

A hoarse yell jolted him and he sat up, bleary-eyed and half awake. The light fell on the ground differently now, and he realized he must have fallen asleep for some time. Shaking his head to clear his muddled senses, he tried to get his bearings. Several disciples were scattering from the edge of the clearing, where an unfamiliar man stood. As soon as David saw him he flinched; the skin on his arms prickled as he struggled to his feet.

The man wore garments that looked like they had been flayed by a whip, with large sections torn away and slices through the fabric. His hair hung in matted locks, except for a few patches of baldness where hair had been ripped out. He held a sharp, pointed stone in his hand like a knife. David saw James holding his forearm, which bled. There was red on the stone.

David was at the opposite end of the clearing from the stranger. He saw all the disciples surging toward him, away from the man.

"Run, David!" Simon urged, pulling at his arm. "The man has demons!" David stumbled back, yanked by Simon, but when Simon let go he stopped moving, watching the stranger with dread fascination.

He noticed the only other figure who had not run away was Yeshua. The teacher stood straight and still. Then he spread his hands as if to embrace the man. "Welcome!"

"What are you doing here?" the stranger shouted, advancing. He staggered, as if he stood aboard the swaying deck of a ship.

"Waiting for you," Yeshua replied. "I have longed for this day. Come, Silas."

The man writhed and crumpled to the ground, hands pressed against his ears. "No, we do not use that name, stop it!"

Yeshua took a step forward. "That is his name; I am not talking to you. Silas! Come to me."

With a painful looking motion the man lurched to his feet and pushed his hair out of his eyes. David saw the man's face and shuddered. The face was somehow shifting through what seemed not only expressions but entire physical countenances – different shapes and features. The faces were in turns woeful, enraged, mocking. But David saw, deeper down, a steely determination flash in the eyes that he sensed was born of some desperate hope. And for all his unsteadiness and jerking limbs, the man's movements brought him more or less toward Yeshua. As David watched, the man tottered toward Yeshua like a little child taking its first steps. Yeshua stood before him with outstretched arms, like a proud parent waiting to receive him.

The man's legs gave out a few paces from Yeshua. He fell to his knees, rocking slowly, muttering.

"Silas, look at me," Yeshua said.

The man struggled to lift his gaze to Yeshua's face, and their eyes met. The man smiled, then immediately his body convulsed and his arm flew up to cover his face. A wail of anguish shook him. "What have you to do with us, Son of God?" his raw voice croaked.

David's eyes widened.

"Be quiet. Come out of him!" Yeshua said. His voice was low and soft, yet sounded with an authority like thunder.

Another convulsion shook the man, then he went limp. David's fear left him. Whatever frightening presence had been in the clearing was now gone.

Yeshua knelt and gently touched the man's shoulder. The figure cringed.

"Silas," he said, his voice tender.

The man was sobbing softly. "They're gone," he whimpered. He appeared very weak, hardly able to push himself from the ground, drained from the struggle he had gone through to get to Yeshua. The teacher pulled him up into his arms and the man wept on his shoulder.

David watched in silence as Yeshua knelt with the man, whispering comforting words too quiet for any but the man to hear. They stayed like that for several minutes, during which the disciples came back to stand around them. When the man shakily got to his feet, the disciples stepped back fearfully.

"All is well," Yeshua said, smiling at the man. "This is Silas."

The man wiped his face and looked around, and David was astonished how gentle and sweet a face he truly had. His eyes were blue and much clearer than they had been, with a quiet strength in them. Yet a shadow seemed to darken his features. He looked like he expected this good freedom to be snatched away from him, a lovely dream from which he must soon wake.

Silas was given a new set of clothes. When he had changed, they saw to caring for his wounds and helped him shave his head. It was getting toward evening, so they made a fire, settling down around it and eating the food from their stores. Yeshua sat next to Silas and encouraged him to speak. He shared about his life before he had been "overtaken," as he called it. It had been a dark life, and he had seen terrible things. But he had found comfort in music, especially in singing, and in wandering outdoors to be in the calming presence of nature.

"I have always loved the forests. But these last years, driven from society by those … those voices…" He sighed and Yeshua put a steadying hand on his knee. "I *lived* in the forests, and every moment was a wicked one. I could not even sing; if I did it frightened me more than being silent."

Yeshua gazed at Silas intently. "Why don't you sing for us now?"

Silas looked down, his eyes glancing from side to side warily. "I don't ... I don't think that would be a good idea."

"Silas."

The sound of his name, spoken in Yeshua's rich voice, drew Silas to lift his head halfway, listening.

"It will help you."

Silas closed his eyes. He sat still for a moment, then nodded. He sat up straighter, took a breath, and began to sing.

Those who were carrying on side conversations hushed, and those who were eating forgot their food. Everyone sat quietly, caught up in the rising notes of Silas's song. The first few notes were shaky, but then something changed and the melody found its strength, unfolding like a flower in the sun. David noticed he knew the words. It was a psalm of King David, and it spoke of deliverance and of the great, vast love of God. David looked through the fire at Silas. Tears were running down his cheeks, and his hands were lifted. Through his song of praise, a last remnant of his captivity was being broken off him, and his chains were falling away. He was a man set free, and now even he was coming to know it.

His song ended, and he fell gently against Yeshua, weeping, as the last notes hovered in the air and the firelight. Yeshua held him close, his eyes shining with tears.

The next morning David woke to find Silas gone. When he asked, Simon informed him that he had seen Silas and Yeshua talking very early. They had embraced and Silas had taken his leave, looking back over his shoulder several times, smiling and shaking his head.

"It is often like that," Simon said. "Yeshua often sends people he has healed back to their own towns so that they can tell what they have experienced, what he has done for them."

"I suppose that draws crowds."

Simon sighed. "Yes, we should be overrun with people at any time now."

They sat quietly for a few minutes, reflecting on the previous day. Then David remembered what had troubled him. "Simon," he asked carefully. "Yesterday, those were demons, yes?"

"Yes."

"And Yeshua seemed to have power over them, yes?"

"He did. He does."

David cleared his throat. "And… the demons, they called him 'Son of God.'"

Simon nodded.

"You do not seem surprised by this."

Simon shrugged. "I am not."

David felt uneasiness twinge in his gut. "And *why* does that not surprise you?"

Simon glanced away uncomfortably for a moment under the interrogation. "Because he is."

"Is what?"

Simon looked back at David. "Yeshua is the Son of God."

David got slowly to his feet. "Simon, you should be very careful. Such a statement is blasphemy."

Simon stood as well. "It is not blasphemy; it is the truth."

David covered his mouth. He thought back to what Andrew had said that first day, at the house of the supposed former paralytic, the way he had spoken of Yeshua. The qualms he had felt then joined with the mounting fear that now filled him. He glared at Simon. "Why did you not tell me earlier?" he demanded.

"He told us not to."

"Who? Yeshua?"

"That is correct." It was Yeshua, from his seat nearby. He was casually leaning against a tree, his eyes calm and untroubled.

"But why? And why did you stop the demon once it said that?"

Yeshua spread his hands. "I want people to get to know me, and learn who I am for themselves. Also, when demons say things, people tend to get frightened, and it is not the right of an unclean spirit to give away who I am. It is my decision when to reveal myself to someone."

David swallowed and sat down again.

Yeshua smiled at him kindly. "It will all make sense in time, David." He tossed him a food sack. "Here, breakfast."

David sat, eating mechanically, while Simon and Andrew talked to him about the first time each of them had realized Yeshua's true identity. They were so excited to discuss it, saying they had been waiting for the moment when it was allowed for them to do so.

As he chewed, half-listening, David considered his options. He made up his mind: he would play things calm, as if he were coming to terms with what had been shared. Then, at the next town, he would quietly go his way, perhaps when Yeshua was teaching a large crowd. He would slip away, and go inform the local priest of the presence of a dangerous sect. They would pass word to Jerusalem, and perhaps the Sanhedrin would get word of it and do something about it.

But… could he really do that? He gazed at the people around him. They were full of joy, that strange, deep joy that had drawn him in the first place. And this man did seem to have something anointed about him. After all, he had sent those demons out of Silas the previous day. Maybe David would wait, listen, and watch longer. Perhaps the man was a prophet. But a prophet who claimed to be God's son? That could not be right. … Could it? David's insides felt twisted. He could not just sit by and watch forever. Information had been placed in his hands. He would need to make a decision. After a few more chews, he decided he would wait until they reached the next town, then go tell the local priest. The rest would be out of his hands.

He glanced over at Yeshua, who was chuckling at something John was saying. His laughing eyes met David's, and David's stomach clenched. It would be difficult to turn this man in. He knew that Yeshua cared deeply for his followers and counted the men around him now his closest friends. He would hate to turn in such a genuine and kind man, even if he was delusional.

But what if he's not delusional? What if what they are saying is true?

The thought overwhelmed and scared him. No. Yeshua was delusional, if kind, and that was the end of it. David sighed, shook his head, and tried to wholly turn his attention to the remnants of his breakfast.

A little later Yeshua stood and told them to pack, that they were going to a nearby town. David swallowed. This was coming sooner than he had anticipated.

"How far away is this town?" he asked.

"Less than a day's walk," Yeshua said. "We should be there by nightfall if we set a good pace." He smiled at David.

David smiled back before looking away.

As the group set out, someone struck up a song and everyone sang along, several walking abreast with their arms across each other's shoulders. David sang too, wincing at the off-key bellowing coming from Simon, and realized he was going to miss traveling with them. He thought of how his life had been before Simon invited him to hear Yeshua speak. Although it had not felt it then, it seemed so lonely to him now. It would be hard to go back to that after this was over. He reflected that he probably would not have friends in Simon and Andrew after this if he betrayed their leader. His heart sank. But he had to do it. It was the right thing, wasn't it? That little nagging thought of *what if* persisted, but he shoved it down again. He could not think about that. He focused on putting one foot in front of the other and listening to the singing and laughter of the others, resolving to enjoy their company while he could.

5

And God Is Good

The afternoon grew hotter, to the point where the road ahead shimmered with the heat and objects in the distance flickered and danced in the eye. Conversation died down and the main focus seemed to turn to getting to their next destination. A drink sack was passed around and David was never so glad for a few mouthfuls of cool water. He wiped the excess from his lips and smeared it on his face with a sigh of relief. As he passed the sack on to Bartholomew an eerie wail rose from the road somewhere ahead of them. It startled him so badly he dropped the sack and had to retrieve it. There were gasps and murmurs among the disciples; several heads swiveled in different directions, trying to spot the source of the mysterious cry that still rose and fell on the dry air. A fair distance ahead of them a small crowd was beginning to gather.

Yeshua sent Mark on ahead and the young man leaped away like a gazelle. He returned shortly and reported to the teacher, pointing at the growing crowd down the road. David couldn't make out what they said, but he saw Yeshua nod and begin moving purposefully forward, angling his body in a way that made it clear he meant to go to the crowd and whatever was taking place there. Everyone behind him quickened the pace to keep up and started talking among themselves.

"I didn't hear, Simon, what is it?" David asked.

His friend's face was difficult to read. "They say that a little girl has died. Her family was resting on their way and she was playing along the road. A bird flew out of the scrub and scared her, and she fell and hit her head on a rock. She was dead before her mother got to her."

David's heart sank. "So sudden," he mumbled.

Simon nodded, his eyes thoughtful.

"Why is Yeshua going to them, Simon?" David asked.

"I do not know, perhaps to offer comfort." He turned his gaze ahead and did not speak further.

They arrived at the edge of the crowd. Yeshua hardly broke stride as he plunged straight into the midst of the people. His disciples followed. David went with them, uneasy at the questioning and indignant looks from those they passed.

Andrew apparently recognized someone and went over to him. "Luke, is it true?"

The man called Luke nodded, his brow heavy. "Yes, I was passing by when I heard the commotion. Someone in the crowd recognized that I was a physician, and the parents begged me to examine the girl. So I did, though I could tell just by looking at her. She is gone." He cleared his throat and shifted on his feet, looking down.

An angry shout broke out somewhere ahead and to the left, at the front of the crowd. "Get back, give them space to grieve!"

Simon emerged out of the throng, his expression intense and strangely excited. "David, come." He took David by the elbow and threaded back through the crowd until they stood at the front edge, where a semicircle of space had been left between those gathered and the bereft family.

The child's mother sat in the dust, cradling a small form in her arms and rocking back and forth. It was from her that the wailing came. Each heart-wrenching cry seemed to be ripped from her body. Her eyes were squeezed shut; she did not seem to be aware of anyone around her. A little distance away the father huddled on the ground, his hands over his face, silent.

The woman moved her arm and David saw the child's face for the first time. There was blood in her hair and on the side of her face, and her eyes were open, staring sightlessly at the sky. David's skin prickled and his hair stood on end, even as a lump formed in his throat. He murmured, "Simon, I don't want to see this." He turned to look at his friend, but Simon was watching Yeshua.

A few paces in front of the mother, a man stood with his arms spread. He was trying to block Yeshua from reaching the woman. "Get back, you! Can you not see these people are in pain?"

Yeshua's face was calm and his voice reassuring. "Peace, friend. I mean no harm." He placed a hand on the man's shoulder and strangely, the man relaxed, stepping aside.

Yeshua knelt down in front of the grieving woman. He laid a hand on the woman's shoulder and she opened her eyes, her wail subsiding into a soft whimper. Then her gaze focused on Yeshua's face. She spoke. "I know you. You are Yeshua. I—I have heard you speak."

"And I know you, Anna," Yeshua said. "I know you have heard me. I am so glad you made the journey to see me." He paused, dipping his head to look deeper into her eyes. "I also know you have seen me help others." He paused, the air between them laden with meaning.

The woman seemed bewildered; her eyes cast about on the ground. "Yes, I have… I don't…" Then a sob escaped her, and she held out her child's body to Yeshua with trembling arms.

Yeshua sat cross-legged on the ground and gently moved the child to his lap. He placed his hand on the woman's cheek, smiling at her as a tear slipped down his face. Then he looked down at the girl and dabbed the blood from her face with his sleeve. He took one of her small hands in his.

"Come awake, little one. We're all waiting for you."

The silence was complete. No one breathed.

And then, from Yeshua's lap, came a quick intake of breath and a delighted giggle. The little girl sat up and flung her arms around Yeshua. The mother scrambled to her knees and fell into them, hugging them both and crying out, and the crowd broke into an uproar and surged forward, hiding them from sight.

David staggered backward, bumping into people who were rushing past him. Shouts of joy filled the air. He nearly fell over the child's father, who was still kneeling on the ground in silence. The man slowly raised his head from his hands, and David swallowed when he saw the man's eyes. They reminded him of how the girl's eyes had been moments ago. But David saw a faint flicker of life begin to glow in the father's eyes as he became aware of the sounds of celebration around him. The man got shakily to his feet, staring at the crowd. Over all the noise the girl's sweet, happy giggle could be heard.

"My child…" the man breathed.

Luke ran back to them and grabbed the man's arm, beaming. "Friend, your child lives! Yeshua has raised her to life again!" He had to support the man as he led him forward. David watched, saw the crowd part, and heard the little girl squeal. "Papa!" The sound of the father's weeping rose into the air to mingle with the rest of the jubilant cacophony.

David wandered back in a daze to the edge of the gathering. A few of the travelers had opened their saddlebags and were passing around raisin cakes in celebration. Several others contributed further provisions, and it became clear that there was going to be a small impromptu feast to toast the little girl's resurrection. Simon found David and seized him in a powerful embrace, his face aglow with wonder. He laughed in David's ear. "I knew he would do it! I did not want to assume, but I still knew he was going to raise her! Incredible! What a day to be with us, David!" He let David go and held him at arm's length. "What have you to say of all this, friend?"

David cleared his throat and licked his lips. He had to clear his throat again and try several times before he could speak. "But she was … you saw? She … and then he … then …" Words failed him. He gestured weakly.

Simon clapped him on the back. "I know! Is it not the most remarkable thing you have ever seen?"

David's legs felt weak. He sat down quickly, thumping to the ground. Simon plopped down beside him, laughing. He motioned to another of the disciples. "Philip! David is doing just what you did the first time the master performed a miracle." The man called Philip looked at David and shrugged with a grin. "It is an appropriate response, wouldn't you say?"

David avoided Philip's eyes and said nothing. He was attempting to maintain some sense of composure, but now that the initial shock had passed he wanted nothing more than to run, if only he would stop shaking. He was terrified. His ears rang and his breath came in short gasps as he tried to make sense of it. What had he just seen? A young girl, dead. He had seen her body, motionless, her eyes devoid of life. He had seen the tracks of tears on the mother's face, the twist of anguish ruining her features. The man Luke had even confirmed the child was deceased.

And … he had seen that same girl alive again. He had witnessed Yeshua take her hand and call to her, like a father calling to his daughter. And now that same child who had lain in the cold silence of death was alight with warmth and life, squirming in her mother's arms, impatient to run about with the other children as her mother clung to her in disbelieving joy.

David wanted to join in the excitement around him, but he was just so afraid. Who was this man, this Yeshua, that death itself turned back to life at his word? David's soul trembled. What was it the demon had said? "What have you to do with us, Son of God?" And it had been speaking to Yeshua.

He peered over at Yeshua out of the corners of his eyes, fearful even to look at him. The teacher was talking with Andrew and several others who crowded about him. Something must have alerted him, because he looked up and stared straight at David. Sweating with fear, David felt himself compelled to turn his head until he was staring Yeshua full in the face.

David's heart skipped a beat as their eyes met. A chill swept through him, and everything seemed to slow, then stop. Those eyes. He was not staring into the eyes of a mere man from Nazareth. The demon was right, and Simon was right. This was the Son of God. David felt he would faint with dread.

Then Yeshua smiled, as if he knew what David was thinking, and it was as if the sun burst through a thick cloudbank. David knew this man. Images flashed in his mind: Yeshua playing with the children that first day on the hillside; Yeshua healing the sick; Yeshua joking with the disciples around a late night fire; Yeshua saying goodbye to Ari.

Suddenly through the fear David knew joy, a joy deeper and more meaningful than anything he had experienced. This was the Son of God. And he was a good man. The child Yeshua had raised broke away from her mother, ran over to Yeshua, and jumped into his arms. As he swung the little girl around in the air, both of them laughing uproariously, David's breath caught in his throat, and a tear pricked his eye. And God was good.

He felt a nudge at his shoulder. He looked up and saw John. The young man had a raisin cake in his hand and a slight smile on his face. He handed David the raisin cake and was about to speak when the father of the girl called for everyone's attention.

"Please, friends!" he said in a loud voice. He stood with his arms around his wife and little girl. His face had changed. Now his eyes shone as they squinted above cheeks bunching from the biggest smile David had ever seen. His wife stood beside him, radiant in the splendor of her joy. Yeshua had resurrected not only a girl, but an entire family. "Please, come join us at our home for supper this evening," the father said. "It is the least we can do – the very least," he added, looking at Yeshua, who nodded graciously. The father kissed his wife on the forehead and took his girl into his arms. He started walking at an energetic pace. "Follow us! We have sent someone ahead to prepare!"

By the time the merry company arrived at the house, extended family had gathered and were preparing a delicious meal. Yeshua, as the guest of honor, was offered the best seat at the table. He declined, saying the little girl should sit there, as she was the one whose resurrection they were celebrating. She wanted to sit with him, however, so together they both chose a place and everyone fell in around them. Soon the food was brought out, and as the dishes were passed so were the stories, as people from the crowd who had better views of the miracle described it to those who had been in the back. It made for enjoyable listening, for it seemed that every few minutes from a different location a voice would exclaim "A miracle!" or "Praise be to God!" or "I wish I would have been up front!"

In the middle of it all sat David, awash in wonder and heady with happiness. His heart burned with his revelation about Yeshua. This depth and breadth of good news was so new to him that he didn't quite know what to do with himself. Several times he dropped what he was holding and he nearly spilled his drink twice. It was like his senses were on high alert.

Eventually his thrill smoothed into a deep sense of awe and contentment. He gazed about him at the glowing faces around the table. Each life had been touched today, in some way, by what Yeshua had done. David looked over and saw his teacher, who he had realized today to be the Son of God – the man who was playing a game with wooden animals with the little girl snuggled on his lap. How it could be, David did not know. But he knew it was the truth.

As he sat at the table he picked out the faces of Yeshua's disciples. Simon, laughing with Andrew and Thomas at some joke he had just told and fancied to be hilarious. James, John, and Bartholomew, talking with the little girl's father and mother in earnest tones, the parents holding hands. The other disciples, speaking with those who had been in the crowd. David saw a light in these men's faces that somehow reflected what he was feeling. It was like they were fuller, more awake, than those around them. He wondered whether, if he spent more time with Yeshua, his face would glow with that same light.

Eventually people began to move back from the table and split into smaller groups in conversation. Torches were lit as the sun set and dusk settled over the party. David was content to watch, still basking in the warmth of the evening.

As the air around him grew cooler, however, so did his disposition. David began to feel a slight prickle in his emotions. He watched the disciples. No matter with whom from the crowd or the girl's family they were talking, they seemed relatively relaxed and confident, and most sat with at least one other of Yeshua's followers. He also noticed the looks passing between Yeshua and his friends, secret laughter and knowing expressions that, even when they were part of separate conversations, tied them together in fellowship. But David was sitting by himself, on the edge of the gathering. He began to wonder if he was such a part of them after all. He recalled the night Ari had left, how there had seemed to be shared connection between himself and Yeshua. He had felt appreciated then, part of an inner circle. Now he just felt left out.

"David?"

He started. It was John. The young man offered him a cup of steaming drink as he sat down beside him.

"Getting a little chilly," John said, smiling.

David tried to smile back. "Yes, it is getting a little cool out here."

The young man nodded. "You know, sitting here, at the edge of things, don't you feel a little left out?"

David slurped his drink in surprise. He wiped his mouth carefully, trying to judge what best to say. "Uh, well … no, no this is fine."

John shrugged. "All right. I just wanted to come tell you to feel free to move closer." He made as if to get up.

"John…" David said, putting a hand on the man's arm. "You can stay, if you want."

John grinned. "So you were feeling left out!"

"No! I just…" David grimaced and dipped his head. "Fine, you're right. It is just that… I am watching you all, and seeing how close you all are with Yeshua. I ..." He fell quiet, unsure if he wanted to admit what was burdening him.

John sat quietly, giving him space.

"I wish I was close to Yeshua, too." David hated that he said it, but he felt relieved at the same time. He glanced cautiously at John, and he saw John smiling at him.

"Why don't you talk to Yeshua about it?"

"What?" David blurted. "I could never do that!"

John tilted his head. "Why not?"

David stared at the young man, studying him incredulously. Was it possible that John did not know about Yeshua's identity? If that was the case, he had no idea how to break the news to the young man, or even if it were his place to share such information at all. "Because … you know… Yeshua is, uh…"

"The Son of God?"

John said it so casually that David flinched and glanced around to see if they had been overheard. He turned back to John and saw with confusion and some annoyance that he was grinning again.

"Yes, that," David said carefully. "And so," he quickly added. "You see why I cannot just go talk to him."

John nodded knowingly. "Ah, I see. You think that being the Son of God makes Yeshua unapproachable."

David spread his hands. "Yes! Do you not recall the entirety of our history? The Lord is holy! Even the high priest can only go behind the curtain in the Most Holy Place once a year to make atonement for us. We are sinful, and God is pure. We are forever separated from the Lord."

"And has Yeshua ever turned you away?"

David froze. "Well, no." He paused. "To tell the truth, he has actually approached me."

John smiled. "Exactly. It is the same with myself and the others. He approached each of us. He invited each of us to follow him."

David thought back to Simon's words during their very first conversation. "A command and an invitation," he muttered.

John nodded. "I do not know how it all works, David. I only know that I have been called by name by Yeshua, the very Son of God, and I follow him. I have not done everything right in my life…" A shadow passed over his face and he glanced down, wincing at some painful memory. "No, I have done many things wrong. I have hurt others… But, somehow, he forgives me." As he said those words, that warm smile spread over his face again, and the shadow passed. His eyes shone. "And he loves me. Me! John! Who would have thought it? John, a disciple Yeshua loves." He placed a hand on David's shoulder. "He is calling you, too. The fact that you now know who he is is itself proof that you need to talk with him."

David looked back to the table. Yeshua was looking at him, and he could almost feel an invitation being extended, to come nearer and know him better. *That's what I want,* he thought. It was the deepest desire of his heart, to be as near to Yeshua as he could get.

"When should I talk to him?" David asked, still looking at Yeshua.

"Once we leave and find a place to settle for the night," John said, "we will likely have a fire and talk for a while. Yeshua usually goes off by himself for a bit after that. I would talk to him then."

He turned to John. "I think I will. Thank you."

"Of course."

They turned back to watch the others. David thought of the conversation to come and hoped what John said was true. With a prick of anxiety, David knew he would find out, one way or the other, later that night.

6

Beloved

The talk lasted much longer than David had anticipated, well into the darkening hours of the night. Gradually the other guests drifted off to their own lodgings, until Yeshua, the disciples, and the girl's family were the only ones remaining at table. At last Yeshua stood, and everyone intuitively understood it was the end of the evening. With a fond final hug with the little girl and warm words to her parents, Yeshua led the way from the house. David turned and watched the family extinguishing the lanterns and torches around the festive board, settling the house and table into peaceful darkness. He looked forward again and took Simon's arm for guidance as his eyes adjusted.

Yeshua and his friends walked for a while under the light of the stars. Few words were spoken; a gentle stillness lay over the land.

They came to a pleasant open space, a clearing with plenty of soft grass and a burbling stream that twinkled in the moonlight. Yeshua said they would spend the rest of the night there, and the men gratefully flopped down and began preparing for sleep. David waited nervously, hoping someone would suggest a fire and conversation, and so delay the conversation he knew he must have with Yeshua. No one did; all were full of food and ready for slumber. The air was warm and heavy, like a cozy blanket tucking them in. One by one the disciples curled up on the grass and fell asleep. David hunched over his knees, painfully awake, fretful. Within minutes he heard the first snores, Simon's loudest among them.

He sighed quietly and looked over toward Yeshua. The teacher had gone off a little way by himself. He sat on a small hill, a dark shape outlined against the stars. Swallowing his fear, David gathered himself and walked over.

"Yeshua?" he said.

He could tell Yeshua looked his way from the gentle glint of his eyes in the starlight. "Yes?"

"I... I was wondering if you and I could talk." A peculiar and sharp fear of rejection suddenly spiked in his chest. What if Yeshua said no? The thought hadn't crossed his mind before; he felt a fool for not having considered it.

Yeshua made a sound of pleasant agreement, moved over, and patted the space beside him. "Sit with me."

David sat. He cleared his throat, pulled at the hem of his sleeve, and fidgeted with the grass. As they sat without speaking, time seemed to stretch painfully between each breath. David found he did not know what to say at all. He felt foolish, tense, and slightly nauseated. But from what he could tell, Yeshua was completely comfortable with the silence. He stole sideways glances and saw him gazing up at the stars. Their light fell on his tranquil, honest face, and David loved him for his serenity.

In the quiet, David noticed the sound of the stream. Was this the same clearing where they had met Silas? He had lost sense of direction at some point during the wild events of the day. At the memory of Silas David recalled his horror just that morning about the idea of Yeshua being the Son of God, and his determination to turn him in. Shame flooded him. He wondered for the second time that day if Yeshua knew, and he reasoned he must. Panic prickled his skin. *He knows!* In his shock and fear he began to stand up. He could make an excuse about going to relieve himself and then just run. Then his ears caught again the trickling of the stream.

That sound brought a memory so sudden and vivid that it seemed to David to float in the air before him. It was a moment from his boyhood, one of many, of fishing the rivers with his father. A sense of peace wrapped around him and he closed his eyes, leaning into it. He remembered those days. The brightness dancing on the water and dazzling his eyes, the warmth of the sun on his back, his father's laughter. It never mattered then what worries or problems he brought to his father, what fears or failures. He was always listened to with kindness, and everything seemed better once it was spoken aloud. He always had felt loved and accepted.

Returning to the present moment, he breathed deeply, strengthened by the memory. Maybe Yeshua would be forgiving, understanding, like his father had been. He had seen Yeshua like that with others. And like John had pointed out, the teacher had never turned him away before. Perhaps everything would be all right.

There was a sweet scent in the air, and a soft breeze caressed his cheek. Light from the brilliant stars cascaded from the sky down the hillsides and lit the blades of grass with a silvery radiance. Zephyrs ruffled the natural carpet into rippling waves of dark and light. The peace from his memory mingled with the tranquility of the clearing, and he felt himself able to speak at last.

"What do you want to say to me?" Yeshua asked.

It was time. But how should he even start? "I… Today was incredible."

Yeshua nodded. "It was."

His turn again. He swallowed and felt his heartbeat quicken. He couldn't come to the point, not yet. "I have never seen anything like it. What happened was… miraculous."

"Mm. It was a very good day."

He opened his mouth, but all that came out was a soft puff of breath. He knew he needed to tell Yeshua what he had considered doing that morning, before the walk and the girl.

But ... what if John was wrong? The young man didn't know that David had almost turned Yeshua in to the authorities as a heretic. What if Yeshua hated him? Yeshua likely already knew and so already hated him, but he had not shown it yet. Would it not perhaps be better to go on pretending everything was fine? What if David spoke the truth, it came out into the open air, and Yeshua officially acknowledged and condemned David's sin and cast him out into the dark on his own? He squeezed the hem of his sleeve, trying to overcome the spiraling of his thoughts, and strained to pick up the stream over the sound of his beating heart. He let out a very slow, measured breath. *Dear God, please have mercy.*

"I almost betrayed you, Yeshua." The words spoken, David felt tears welling in his eyes. "But I didn't know! I swear I didn't know."

A hand, gentle and reassuring, rested on his shoulder. That touch – kind, without a trace of anger. It almost hurt worse than a slap. David hunched away wretchedly and buried his face in his hands, sobbing. All the shame, all the confusion, all the fear came out in his weeping. "Forgive me!" he managed through his sobs.

Yeshua's arm was around him, and he felt himself being pulled near. He was weeping into Yeshua's chest like a little child. "I am so sorry," he repeated over and over. "I am so sorry. I thought… I thought you were a heretic." He sniffed and wiped at his eyes. He wanted to pull back and look for Yeshua's expression, but he was still afraid what he might see. So he remained leaning against him, looking down. "I thought it was my duty, I thought you were turning people from God." He paused. "No… I did wonder if it might be true. I thought, somehow, it might be. But the thought frightened me too much,

I would not entertain it. But after today, I know." He felt a shiver roll down his spine. He sat up and turned to face Yeshua. He couldn't see the teacher's face completely, but the moonlight showed him the glint of his eyes. He felt he owed it to Yeshua to look him in the eyes as he said what followed, no matter how it terrified him. "Now I know that you are the Son of God." He stared wide-eyed into the dark, trying and yet afraid to see Yeshua's reaction.

The shadow over Yeshua's face split as the moonlight caught his broad smile. "My brave David." Yeshua hugged him, and David felt that he was being poured into, like a dry and dusty cup that is being filled with water fresh and sparkling from a spring. In that embrace he felt a new level of Yeshua's love and approval. He also felt that Yeshua had an exultant pride in him in this moment. David began crying again, utterly undone. How could God, how could Yeshua, approve of him? How could he feel pride in him? What love was this?

"All I needed," Yeshua said in his ear, "was for you to start. I just needed you to come to me, to unburden yourself, to admit what was killing you inside. I want you to remember this: I am always here. All I ever need is for you to begin."

They pulled apart again, and Yeshua placed his hands on David's shoulders. "I know how hard that was for you to do. I love your bravery, David."

David sat back, moved by Yeshua's love and his words, feeling lighter and yet fuller in heart than he could remember being. It did not even feel as dark in the clearing as it had been. The moon and stars seemed to be giving more light. He found he could see Yeshua's face clearly now. "And you forgive me?"

"I do."

He sat quietly, taking it in. Then he chuckled at the reality of his strange situation. "I am sitting here, having a conversation with the Lord. That… I am not certain my mind can comprehend it."

Yeshua smiled, and David saw there were tears in his eyes. "And I am sitting here, spending time with my beloved friend. I have waited so long for these moments with you, David."

David stared. "You have?"

Yeshua wrapped his arms around his knees, gazing up at the heavens. "Oh yes, longer than I can tell. So long, in fact, that when my father and I designed the world, we created this clearing for you, in preparation for tonight."

David thought he must have misheard. "Did – did you say you created this clearing for *me*?"

"Yes! We knew you would be so anxious and burdened that you would need the memory of your father's love and patience to calm you, to give you the bravery you needed to speak to me."

David's heart fluttered and his jaw dropped. "But how did…" He stopped himself as Yeshua looked at him. "Of course, yes, you knew that I thought about that."

Yeshua gave him an understanding smile and pointed in the direction of the stream. "We placed the stream there, so that you would hear it in that moment you almost left, so that the memory would come to you just when you needed it." He spread his arms toward the sky. "We aligned the motions of the heavenly bodies and the direction and strength of the breeze and the current length of the grass and the exact tilt of that tree over there so that the leaves, wind, light, and grass would move together in just such a way that we knew would set you at ease, so that you could find the words to start the conversation we are having now." He grinned and crossed his arms. "Fairly impressive, yes?"

Chills were running over David's whole body. He suddenly felt so very small, and yet so very seen, all at once. *For me? All this for me? Who am I?*

"I am telling you all this," Yeshua said, looking intently at David, "so that you know how important you are to me. David, I know you do not think much of yourself. But you are everything to me. I have loved you all your life. I know the burdens and pains you carry, and I crafted this moment for you, set in motion since the dawn of the world, because I longed for you to talk to me. I needed you to come to me, so that you and I could understand each other, and our friendship could truly form. I have longed that you would believe in me, so that you can be with me and my father." He smiled, and there was a quiver in his voice. "I need you to know how greatly you are loved, David, by me and by the father. You were named well. Even that was prepared for you. 'David,' meaning 'beloved.' You are precious to me. I love you."

Tears were streaming down David's face, and he did not bother to brush them away. He just sat there, soaking in every word Yeshua spoke. He was seen. He was known. He was *beloved* of God. The God who created the stars not only knew him, but that God had actually pursued him, had come down to earth to meet with him, and had carved out a special space and time for him – this very moment. It was all so beautiful, too good to be true. And yet it was true. Yeshua's hand was on his shoulder. It was real.

After some moments had passed, David asked, "Is that why you allowed the little girl to die? So that I would watch you raise her and discover who you are?"

"Yes, partly." Yeshua smiled. "I also needed her mother to know me as not only a teacher far away, high on a hill just within sight, but the very close, very real healer who knows her sorrows and is there for her in her time of need. I needed an old man in the crowd that gathered to receive hope that unexpected, glorious things still happen in this life, and a little boy there needed to know that he does not need to be afraid of death, because I will be there for him. These people needed that moment at that very time in each of their stories."

David smiled. "Remarkable."

"Yes," Yeshua replied. "It's amazing to see what comes when lives intersect at just the right time." He smiled at David, and his eyes glinted with something that David felt tempted to call mischief.

"What?" David asked. "What is it?"

"Nothing. You will see."

They talked for a long time after that, and the feeling grew and grew in David that he had found the friend he had been missing his entire life. Yeshua was so warm, so open, and so honest that at times he forgot he was talking to the Lord of creation. He was Yeshua, his greatest and closest friend. He shared things with Yeshua he had never shared with anyone, and as he aired out those rooms in his heart, David felt a darkness lift from him. An oppression he had never realized was there now dissipated, and he felt free. He fell asleep beside Yeshua, not knowing when conversation ended and slumber began.

7

Words of Hope

When David woke the sun was still below the horizon; the bottoms of the clouds blushed with the faintest tinges of pink in the predawn sky. He pushed himself to a sitting position, rubbing his stiff back, watching several silhouettes huddle together off to his right. One of them approached him.

It was Yeshua. He squatted down beside David with a warm smile. "You are awake. Excellent. I want you to go with Peter and Andrew into town today and purchase supplies. One of the water sacks has a hole that needs repair and we need more food. Will you do that for me?"

David nodded, feeling a sense of pride and gratitude that Yeshua would ask anything of him.

The teacher smiled again and placed a hand on his shoulder. "I so enjoyed our talk last night. I love you, my friend."

"I, uh … thank you, Yeshua," David stammered. He wanted to respond in kind, but the words stuck on his tongue and refused to be spoken. He nodded sheepishly.

Yeshua winked at him and David grinned; it was understood. The teacher leaned close conspiratorially. "And while you are out, buy a new cloak for John. He is badly in need of one. But," he added, glancing around, then holding a hand to the side of his mouth. "Don't tell anyone; let it be a nice surprise," he whispered. "Today marks two years since John finished his apprenticeship to a tanner, and though he left his appointment to follow me, I want him to know his accomplishments and sacrifice have not been forgotten. This will be between the two of us until you return, yes?"

David got to his feet, flushed with importance and the shared secrecy, wrapping his own cloak about him in the chill air. "Will do. Not a word." He went to join Simon and Andrew as Yeshua made his way among the other slumbering men, waking them each with a soft word.

"Are we ready?" David asked.

"Almost," Andrew said. "We just need to get the funds from Judas. He keeps the money bag."

The three men walked over to Judas, who was crouching with his back toward them and his hands moving rapidly between two satchels.

"A new day dawns, Judas," Simon said.

The man started and looked up quickly. "Eh?"

"The master sends us off to refresh our supplies," Andrew replied. He held out a hand. "Will you be so generous as to equip us for the task?"

Judas grunted and dropped a few coins into Andrew's hand.

Andrew was not impressed. "Is that all?"

"Find good deals," Judas said shortly.

Andrew sighed and motioned to Simon and David. David let the other men walk off a few paces before turning back to Judas. "Yeshua asked me to purchase something else as well. A few more coins?"

The other man stared suspiciously at David. "Why did he only tell you?" He scrutinized David for several moments.

David's cheeks flushed with irritation. He opened his mouth to inquire angrily at what Judas was implying, when Yeshua appeared at his side. "What he says is true, Judas. Use the money I put in from that small carpentry job I did for Martha's friend in Bethany."

Judas sighed and grudgingly dropped several coins into David's waiting hand.

"Your consideration is greatly appreciated," David said with a sarcastic formal dip of his head.

Yeshua raised an eyebrow.

David coughed. "I mean, thank you, Judas."

The eyebrow returned to its normal height, Yeshua's eyes twinkling with good humor. He clapped them both on the back. "Now go, David, they have started without you!"

David turned to see Simon and Andrew cresting the top of the hill leading out of the little valley. "Wait!" he cried, shoving the coins in his satchel and running after them.

"I understand, but it is Judas's way; try not to take it personally," Simon said as they arrived at the outskirts of the nearest village. The sun was coming into its full morning brightness and their backs were warm with its touch. "He is jealous of his responsibility as the keeper of our money."

David shrugged and laughed. "Andrew, did you ever think your brother would be a peacekeeper?"

Andrew smirked. "Never!"

Simon punched his brother playfully in the arm. "Yes, and when did we ever think we would hear you talking in the presence of more than three people? You used to be so shy!"

"It seems Yeshua has impacted us all," David mused, half-jokingly. He took a deep breath through his nose. "Oh," he said, as his stomach let out a loud rumbling gurgle. "Those spices smell heavenly!"

"Market day!" Andrew agreed, increasing his speed.

They soon reached the main thoroughfare. The streets were clogged with traveling merchants with their carts, while more established vendors hawked their wares from wooden stalls erected along the walls. All were trying to shout down their competition and win the eye and coin of the passersby, of whom there was no shortage. Rich aromas wafted from the pots of the meat sellers, elegant weavings flashed in the sunlight, and music seemed to hover on the air with no clear origin. Nearly every direction one looked hands were waving to get attention and objects of desire were temptingly displayed. Taken in at a moment it was enough to make David dizzy. This place was bursting with life, a thronging commotion at the intersection of business and pleasure.

After making their way deftly through the crowd and ignoring the enticements of several different street vendors, they successfully purchased enough provisions for the next several days. Then they stopped at the cart of a traveling craftsman to get the leaking water sack repaired. As the brothers haggled with the man over the price, David drifted away on his own. He had to find a nice cloak for John. Yeshua had asked him, of course, which was his primary motivation. But John had also been the one the previous evening, taking time away from the festivities, to hear him out and encourage him to speak with Yeshua. He owed the man something as a means of saying thank you. Maybe he would put some of his own money in along with the few coins he had been allotted so that he could get John something of truly good quality.

His eyes roved the sea of merchants and customers until he saw several cloaks hanging from a latticework attached to one of the stalls on the other side of the street. Quickly he wove his way through the jostling bodies and squeezed into a space where he could examine the garments without risk of getting shoved. He rubbed the fabric between his fingers and smiled with satisfaction. One of these would do excellently. Not only were they durable, but the material was lightweight for easy bearing and smooth enough to serve as a comfortable blanket on cooler nights. He turned to the merchant and fished in his satchel for the money.

"How much for one of these?" he asked. He waited for several moments, hand in his satchel. When he did not hear a response, he glanced up. For a moment he could not see anyone behind the counter. Then he spotted a young woman sitting in the corner, wiping her nose and getting hastily to her feet. As she turned toward him he saw her wiping her eyes.

"Yes, sir – one moment and I will be with you."

"Are you all right?" David asked.

"Yes, I'm fine," she said, but it was easy to tell she was lying. She came from behind the counter into the street beside him and indicated the cloaks. "Which of these do you want?"

He then saw that the cloaks were of different lengths. He apologized, saying he needed a moment to consider. David scratched his head, trying to remember how tall John was. But once he decided which cloak would fit his friend best, he still continued acting as if he were scrutinizing the merchandise. He kept glancing at the girl out of the corner of his eye. It was painfully obvious she was choking back tears; every few moments her chest would heave silently and she would breathe in sharply through her nose. David wanted to ask her what was wrong, but he did not know what he would say if she told him or how he could possibly help with whatever it was. He felt at a loss. It was probably best to just buy the cloak and leave.

Then he realized he recognized her. He turned to her. "Pardon me, but weren't you recently in Capernaum? You were staying at an inn with a young man, and you both went out to the hillside to hear Yeshua of Nazareth teach?"

She looked at him in surprise. "Yes, I was. I – we were there." She dabbed at her running nose. "Do I know you, sir?"

He shook his head. "No, I am just a fellow traveler who was there at the same time. We were never introduced." He shifted uncomfortably. "Ah, well I should probably fix that. I am David."

She smiled at him politely. "My name is Rachel. The man with me was my husband, Levi."

"It is nice to see you again." David looked around. "I do not see your husband. Is Levi here as well?"

He knew immediately that it was the wrong question. Rachel's eyes filled with tears; she covered her mouth and shook her head.

David started to sweat. He had messed this up badly. What now?

Rachel cleared her throat and tried to talk. "My husband…" She steadied herself and took a deep breath. "He is very sick. He fell ill four days ago and has been lying on a cot in the charge of a physician in our own little town. I had to come here by myself, for this village has the largest market around, to sell what I can so that I will be able to afford his treatments."

His mouth dry, David fumbled for words. "I am so sorry to hear this."

"Thank you." The girl smiled wanly, her fingers fidgeting with her dress. "Levi is a good man, and I love him. We have not been married long, only last summer, and—" Without warning a great, shaking sob overtook her. "I cannot lose him! I will be alone!"

As Rachel wept openly, David put an arm gingerly on her back. She stepped into him and cried harder, wrapping her arms around one of his as the tears flowed. She gasped in a quick breath. "I apologize, I just…" She clung to his arm.

David saw several heads turning his way. Not knowing what else to do, he guided Rachel back around the counter and sat her down inside the stall. He sat down beside her, letting her hold onto him until she calmed down. As the crying lessened, she let go of him and drew into herself, wrapping her arms around her bent knees. "I am so sorry to trouble you. This fear, it just comes upon me so strongly at times that it is all I can do to bear it. It is like a yawning black pit in my heart, and I feel it will consume me."

David shuddered.

"David? David, where are you?"

Simon. David breathed an inward sigh of relief. Simon and Andrew would be able to help. David scrambled up and poked his head above the wooden counter. He saw Simon and Andrew peering over the heads of the crowd looking for him. Andrew saw him and elbowed Simon, and the brothers made their way over to join them. David met them outside the stall to briefly explain. Then Simon nudged Andrew, who nervously ran his hands over his tunic before going into the stall.

He bent down in front of Rachel, who stared dully at the floor. "Hello Rachel. My name is Andrew." He smiled kindly at her, his eyes soft. "Can we take you back to where you are staying?"

Rachel nodded. "I don't think I will be able to sell anything else today feeling like this, and business has been good so far. I have probably made enough." She moved quietly, folding the cloaks and other garments she was selling and packing them into the bag with her earnings. Then she led them out of the busy market and down several quieter streets.

As the noise of the market grew fainter, the streets got narrower and the buildings seemed to cluster more closely overhead, until it nearly seemed they were walking through tunnels, the tops of the buildings on either side looming over them and casting them into shadow.

Eventually Rachel stopped at the door of what proved to be a cramped and tiny inn. The three men followed her inside. There were no windows, but torches in sconces on the wall, coupled with a fire in a small hearth, lit the main room with flickering light.

"Please, sit for a moment, sirs," Rachel said. She moved toward a man who looked to be the innkeeper. "I will order us some refreshments."

Simon moved past her and smiled, motioning for her to take a seat. "This is on us, friend."

She smiled gratefully as he went on to speak with the innkeeper. She sat down at a small table and Andrew and David joined her.

"I do not know why you are showing me this kindness," Rachel said, looking at her hands, then glancing at the men. "But I thank you."

Andrew nodded. "Of course. And do not feel embarrassed for sharing. We are glad to be able to bear this burden with you. Fear is no small enemy, and fear of being alone is terrible."

The girl nodded sadly. "Sometimes I find myself wondering about what will happen, to Levi, to me. What if I cannot make enough money to pay for his treatment? What if he … what if he dies? His mother would be heartbroken." She swallowed. "So would I. And I would be alone. What would become of me?"

Andrew leaned forward, securing her gaze. "I know it is difficult to hear this, Rachel, but do not lose hope. God has not forgotten you. And he will show you that he is with you and help you move forward no matter what happens. We will pray for Levi's recovery from this sickness and for peace for you in the meantime."

"Yes," David said, clearing his throat nervously. "And – And keep your thoughts on the Lord. We are promised through the words of the prophet Isaiah that God keeps us in perfect peace when our minds are fixed on Him, when we trust in Him."

Simon returned with their drinks. Just as David was about to taste his, a man several tables over pushed himself to his feet.

"Wait a minute," he said, looking at Simon and Andrew. "Aren't you two of the ones who were with that Yeshua fellow?"

Simon swallowed a great gulp of his drink and stifled an untimely burp. "Yes, we are followers of Yeshua."

The man grinned widely. "Well this is good timing! I never got out to see your teacher speak because of this bum leg of mine. Come and share some of his teaching with all of us now."

The brothers looked at each other, surprised.

"Come on," the man cajoled. "Share with us. What you were telling that girl there would be a good place to start, I imagine."

Simon turned to Andrew, but Andrew blushed and shook his head. "You go, Simon."

David was confused. Were they really considering doing this? Here? As Simon got up and moved to the front of the room, David leaned over to Andrew. "Why are you humoring that man? He looks as if he has had one too many drinks today."

Andrew smiled and shrugged. "Any time we get an opportunity to teach as Yeshua has instructed us we take it. Why would we ever let one pass us by?"

"Friends," Simon said, and the room quieted. "We are here with you today because Yeshua sent us into town to purchase supplies. But I do not doubt this was no coincidence that we were sent here, today, to your market." He glanced at Rachel and she dipped her head. "We have been discussing fear, particularly fear of the future turning out to be less favorable than we have hoped, and fear of being alone. We have also been speaking of the necessity of making enough money to take care of ourselves and our loved ones."

He spread his hands. "As Yeshua has taught us, so we encourage you: Look at the birds. They do not worry about how they will survive. They live each day just doing what they were created to do, and God provides for them. For us, it is important that we put the Lord God first in our lives, seeking His kingdom before our own desires, even our own necessities. When we do this, our heavenly father will provide for us everything we need."

"To see an example from our history," Andrew put in from his seat at the table, "in the time of wicked King Ahab, God used ravens to feed the prophet Elijah as he served the Lord. God can use anything he pleases to provide for us, no matter how unlikely."

"True, and then Elijah was sent to the widow of Zarephath and both were sustained during the famine as they put the Lord first," David commented, surprised to hear himself contributing anything to the discussion.

Simon grinned broadly. "Yes! As the widow did what the Lord told her to do through Elijah, she and her son were provided for by means beyond which the mind of man can fathom. So you see how he provides for all our needs as we follow his leading." He smiled at Rachel. "When you are worried and feeling overwhelmed, take comfort in the providence of the Lord that you see around you every day. He cares for every living thing. And you are most beloved; you are cherished by the Lord. He will look after you with the greatest care. Elijah thought he was alone, but God showed him he wasn't." Simon caught Rachel's gaze so she knew he was speaking directly to her. "Neither are you."

The girl began to smile. Her bottom lip quivered, but David could see it was hope blooming within her, not the former fear, that caused this emotion.

"Platitudes? Is that really the best Yeshua can do?" scoffed a voice from the side of the group. A youth by the wall stood up and crossed his arms. He scowled at the girl. "You let these trite words of a scruffy fellow from Nazareth encourage you, and you are naïve indeed."

Rachel's eyes lowered.

David saw Andrew sit up straighter, and he saw Simon shift his weight toward the speaker, his expression unreadable.

"Your teacher is nothing more than a peddler of cheap tricks and cheaper words," the young man sneered, lounging against the wall. "And look at who he surrounds himself with – the uneducated and slow-witted. It is no great wonder that you believe his words, fisherman!"

The mood in the room changed abruptly, like a light being snuffed. The inn's patrons sat stiffly in their seats, eyes flitting back and forth between the youth and Simon, watching to see what Simon's response would be.

David's eyes were wide. He looked around nervously. If Simon started a fight here, who would consider his words then? Would Rachel lose this new hope that the truth he had shared had planted? His stomach clenched.

"Friend," he heard Simon say. His voice was calm, like a gentle breeze on still water. David turned his attention back to the front of the room.

Simon stood with his hands spread. "I cannot speak for others who follow Yeshua, but you are right about me."

David's mouth fell open.

"I am uneducated," Simon continued. He indicated his callouses and rough palms. "These hands have seen many days of hard labor. I know my way much better around a fishing boat than I do a scroll. While I would not say I am slow-witted, I am not the sharpest intellect, that is certain." He flashed a smile at David. "Though I know others who have come to Yeshua who are as bright as any scholar you may mention. But Yeshua is no respecter of persons. Any may come to him and hear his words and be saved, be the intellect great or small. It is entirely a matter of having an open and willing heart." He extended his hand to the youth. "Will you come and hear him for yourself? Perhaps then you may make an informed decision."

The youth's smirk faded. He looked around at the many sets of eyes that now rested on him. He shrugged and tried to look as if he were unruffled, but he made his way quickly out the door into the street.

The people murmured among themselves. "Why didn't you put him in his place? The young upstart!" asked an indignant old woman near the front, addressing herself to Simon. All eyes turned back to him.

"I tell you the truth," Simon said slowly, looking around to meet the gaze of every person as he spoke. "It is not up to me to fight to defend myself. I leave that in the hands of the Lord. If we will humble ourselves before God now, he will lift us up in due time. But as I was saying," he said, looking at Rachel again. "Give God all your anxiety. He is safe to trust with your fears and worries, and he has good plans for you. He can give you peace that no circumstance can touch. Don't worry about tomorrow – tomorrow will worry about itself." The group laughed.

David laughed along. *"I tell you the truth."* He smiled. He had heard Yeshua use that phrase often in the time he had known him. It was pleasing to hear Simon use it now.

He wondered at Simon. What his friend had just done— As long as he had known him, Simon had always been quick to lash out in anger. He was stubborn, had his share of pride, and was quick to take offense. These traits, coupled with his hot head and penchant for acting first and thinking later, had gotten him into trouble on more occasions than David could count. Simon was one to trade blows more readily than sort anything out with words.

And yet here, in the flickering light of the fire-lit room, he saw a man transformed. His friend had been mocked by someone intent on causing dissention. The Simon David had grown up with would have rushed upon that young man in a twinkling. But this Simon – the Simon who had sat at the feet of Yeshua – had been humble and kept his head. He had pointed everything back to what was actually important, and made clear the invitation that Yeshua extended to all who would truly listen. This Simon had extended grace to his accuser. It took David's breath away. He nearly felt like crying, it was so beautiful. And all this change from being with Yeshua. David had the distinct feeling, watching Simon now, that in this moment he was seeing Simon as he was meant to be. True, he still had his flare-ups. He was by no means perfect. But he was changing. He was being remade.

Simon spoke for several minutes more, then prayed for a few people who came up to him with requests. David watched with fascination. Then his thoughts returned to the table, and he joined Andrew in talk with Rachel.

He could tell something had changed in her. It was as if hearing of Yeshua and his teachings had turned on a lamp inside her where the yawning pit had been. The darkness had fled, and in its place was a steady, peaceful light, a light which David somehow knew would spread inside her until it overflowed the bounds of her body and gave illumination to others. Her circumstances had not changed. Her husband was still sick, with no guarantee of recovery. But she knew God cared for her. She had told her story, shared her fears, and had been welcomed and told of a love far greater and far truer than the darkest lie fear had ever whispered. She knew now that she was not alone.

Simon joined them and they all talked for about an hour, until Simon stood and declared that the three men had best be going, because their group would be wondering what had become of them. They prayed with Rachel, that God would be merciful to Levi and grant him healing, and that they would both sense his nearness and love for them. When they had ended the prayer, Rachel gave each of them a hug. As David turned toward the door to leave he felt her put a hand on his arm. She handed him a bundle. He shook it out; it was the cloak he had been eyeing for John.

"Please take it," she said, seeing him start to protest. "You have given me so much today."

"Me?" he said, surprised. "What did I do?"

"You saw me," she said simply. "You saw me, and you took the time to ask me if I was all right." She smiled. "I could tell you were frightened, that you didn't know what to say. But you cared enough to say something anyway, and it meant so much." She gestured. "And it led to all this." She hugged him again. "God sent you to me today like he sent the ravens to Elijah, and Elijah to the widow. I know I do not need to fear being alone. You reminded me today that the Lord is with me. Yeshua is with me."

He looked at her, astonished. "You mean, you know who Yeshua is?"

She nodded and smiled playfully. "There are more of us who know him as Lord than you might think. Sometimes we just need to be reminded. Our lives intersected at just the right time."

David smiled. "Goodbye, Rachel."

"Goodbye, David."

As Simon, Andrew, and David walked back, they discussed all that had happened. David shared what he had seen in Simon at the inn, and Simon thanked him, sounding both embarrassed and touched. Just as they were rejoining the others, David was finishing recounting his final conversation with Rachel.

"And then she said that she just had to be reminded, that our lives had intersected at just the right--" He broke off. "…at just the right time." his mouth hung open. He turned, looking for Yeshua, who was leaning nonchalantly against a tree, and ran over to him. "You said that last night!"

Yeshua hid a smile behind his hand, nodding wisely. "Ah, so you understand now."

David scratched his head. "So that was why you said, 'wait and see.' That is … that is … unbelievable. You knew I would meet Rachel today, didn't you? That is why you sent me to get supplies."

Yeshua clapped him on the back. "We also needed food, and it was your turn to pull some weight around here." He grinned and tapped the side of his nose. "But yes, I knew. It's a Son of God thing. What surprised me was how long it took you to make the connection. It was a long walk from town!" He nudged David playfully and they laughed. Yeshua then moved to John and presented him with his new cloak, chuckling with glee at the look of speechless joy and appreciation on the young man's face.

David watched Yeshua and felt deep respect and love burn in his heart. This man was his Lord, his friend, and his teacher. The ache he had felt during the feast after the girl's resurrection, that desire to be near Yeshua, had gained so much strength through their conversation the previous night and through watching him now, that David knew it was becoming one of the chief yearnings of his life. This was God. And God, to his utmost astonishment, not only was approachable, but had sought him out. He was chosen, and he was beloved. David remembered the words spoken to young men who were beginning to follow a teacher: "May you be covered with the dust of your rabbi." And there it was, words put to the zeal rising within him. That was it. That was what he wanted for himself. He wanted to always be so close to Yeshua that the dust kicked up from the road by Yeshua's sandals covered him. He wanted to be near enough to hear

Yeshua's breath and know his bidding before he said it, and to do what he could for him, to serve him.

Yeshua glanced over at David, smiled, and beckoned him over. As they stood admiring John's new cloak, Yeshua squeezed David's shoulder warmly, and David knew his heart's cry was heard and accepted with great joy.

"So," Yeshua said, clapping his hands together and addressing Simon, Andrew, and David. "How was the trip into town? Uneventful, eh? Nothing interesting to report?"

The three grinned at each other. "Not exactly," Andrew said with a chuckle. The others gathered around to hear their tale.

"So there we were, minding our own business, buying supplies," Simon began. "And suddenly we turned around and David was gone! We couldn't find him anywhere. We shouted for him, and then we saw his head pop up from, of all places, behind a merchant's counter…"

8

A Place At His Side

Over the next several days there was much fruitful ministry in which Yeshua did many wonderful miracles, healing the sick and driving out demons. Many came to believe in him. It was a wondrous time. Overall.

David was always brought to the brink of tears when he saw someone make the same conclusion he himself had made, that Yeshua really was the Son of God. Whenever someone came up to him and confessed him as Lord, Yeshua always welcomed them as if he had been waiting all his life for that moment. In fact, David knew, he had. The joy and love that overflowed from Yeshua in those encounters was medicine for the soul – he was utterly fearless in expressing his feelings for these people, his desire that they know him for who he was, his ache for them, and how greatly he rejoiced when they tied themselves to him and expressed their love in return.

For all this wonder, however, David's heart felt tainted. When someone made their confession of faith in Yeshua and he saw how the Master responded to that person, David felt an unpleasant twinge of jealousy. It felt to him almost as if these people were stealing some of Yeshua's love for him, some of the special bond he and Yeshua shared. He had to wrestle with this in silence, for he would not confide his feelings, which he knew instinctively to be wrong, to anyone, not even Simon.

One blazing hot afternoon, he had just squinted through watching a young man confess Yeshua as Messiah. As Yeshua and the young man embraced and stepped aside to talk privately, David turned away, feeling bitter and also ashamed of his bitterness. He walked away from the group and sat down by the edge of the water.

After a few minutes he felt a hand on his shoulder, and he stiffened in embarrassment. Yeshua.

"What's going on, David?" Yeshua asked.

"Nothing," David said. "Just enjoying the breeze off the water."

His friend sat down beside him. "Yes, clearly everything is fine. You look so happy."

David chuckled despite himself.

They sat in silence for a moment, then Yeshua leaned into David's peripheral vision. "So?"

"I'd rather not say."

"Fair enough," Yeshua sighed. "Sit there in your misery."

David winced until he heard the hint of a laugh in the words. "Well, all right. I … I can't help … When others confess you as Messiah, when they come to you as their Lord, and I see how you interact with them…" He trailed off.

"… You think my love for you lessens," Yeshua said, and David cringed. "You think our bond decreases and becomes less special, because I have it with others."

David's cheeks burned with guilt. "I know I shouldn't feel this way," he mumbled, "but I do. That's exactly how I feel."

Yeshua crossed his arms. "You are jealous." He paused, tilting his head reflectively, and then shrugged. "I mean, I can't fault you for it; I am pretty incredible."

David glanced at him and Yeshua shoved him playfully, with a smile that David felt made things somewhat better.

"You're going to have to get used to sharing me," he said, becoming somewhat serious. "I did come to save the whole world, you know. There are lots of Davids out there, people who need my love, people who need my friendship."

David flinched, wounded.

"What I mean by that," Yeshua said, putting his arm around David's shoulder, "is that there are many, many people out there who are feeling the way you used to feel – unseen, hurting, broken. They need the love of the Father, the love I can give to them. They need the love of the One who made them. This should help you feel compassion for them, knowing that they are as you once were – imagine still being in that place of darkness."

In that moment, David did let himself imagine it, and his eyes filled with tears. He thought of his own past, how his heart was before he met Yeshua, how he was filled with only wind and sand, nothing of substance, nothing alive. He thought of himself now. Even though he was feeling somewhat miserable at the moment, he knew that for the first time in his life he was truly living. He knew his heart was full of the love of the Father, expressed in the friendship of the Son. He was part of that family. He *knew* he was loved. He imagined still being lost, and his heart broke for those people who had yet to come to know Yeshua.

David brushed a hand across his eyes and nodded. "I see what you are saying. I will keep a better guard on my emotions in future, Yeshua. I am sorry."

"You are more than forgiven, friend." Yeshua got to his feet. Then he leaned down, put his hands on David's shoulders, and spoke quietly. "And our friendship, yours and mine, is unique. Trust our friendship. My love for each person is special because each person is different, and my heart has more than enough room for everyone. You only gain members in our family when others come to me. Remember that: you only gain. I love you. Now stop crying or people will think I'm being mean to you. I've got an image to upkeep!"

He gave David's shoulder a playful squeeze and went back to the group. David sat there a few moments more, letting the truth soak in to displace his doubts and take deeper root. He would trust Yeshua. He took a deep breath, got to his feet, and rejoined the others, lighter and content.

The next day, David had an encounter that shaped his heart and mission for the rest of his life. It started in the synagogue and ended at a table.

He was just coming from the market with Andrew, having stocked up on supplies for the group. As they had extra time before they needed to be back, Andrew suggested they visit the synagogue. This was the first time David had gone to a synagogue since he realized who Yeshua was. They stood at a little distance, listening to a rabbi teaching from the Torah. As he listened, David was overwhelmed by joyful wonder. It was as if a secret vault had been unlocked, as if his ears had suddenly been opened. As he listened to the teaching all he heard was *Yeshua.* The things that were being read, from thousands of years ago, were clearly pointing to the person of Yeshua. A thrill went through him and he nearly dropped the goods in his arms. And he *knew* Yeshua! The magnitude of where he was, what he was part of, what he was witnessing, nearly drove him to his knees in awe.

He glanced away from the rabbi, laughing to himself in disbelief. He then realized with a jerk that he was looking into the eyes of a Roman soldier, who was standing even further away, completely outside the synagogue. He turned away hurriedly. Something stopped him, though, from turning his attention back to the rabbi. Something in the Roman's eyes looked… hungry. Not hungry like a ravenous wolf, not a frightening hungry. An eager hungry, an intent observational expression. David left Andrew's side, casually strolling away until he too was outside the synagogue. He stood slightly behind the Roman off to one side. He watched the man. The Roman seemed uncomfortable being there, but he was glancing around within the synagogue, as if he were hoping to see something in particular.

"Hey you, Roman!" A group of men stalked over. Several were big and brawny, and a few had knives. "What are you doing hanging around our house of worship?"

David grimaced. These types of interactions never ended well.

The Roman shook his head, like he had been pulled from thought. "I, uh, was just patrolling."

"No you weren't," a youngish man sneered. "You were standing still for a while. It looked like you were listening. Is Roman spying on our teachers now?"

"I was not doing anything of the kind," the Roman said, gritting his teeth. He reached for the sword at his hip. "I advise you all to disperse."

"We advise *you* to disperse, Roman scum!" another man yelled. "There are more of us than you, and this is our synagogue." Weapons were unsheathed.

David saw Andrew notice what was going on and start toward the group of men to try to calm the situation. Before he got there, however, the Roman had walked away, his back straight, to the jeers of the men. David kept his eyes on the Roman. The man stopped a far distance away, but peered back at the synagogue and glanced around down different streets, pacing in what seemed to be irritation and urgency.

For some reason David did not understand, he felt the urge to approach the Roman. He could not explain it, but something inside him identified with the way the man seemed to be trying to appear uninterested but kept glancing back toward the synagogue. Then David realized it reminded him of how he felt that first morning on the hillside when Simon told him Yeshua was leaving for the evening – he did not want to appear dismayed but he really, really wanted to keep listening to Yeshua and follow behind.

David motioned to Andrew and, when Andrew had joined him, explained how he was feeling. Andrew looked at him questioningly, but allowed David to hand him the market items and stood waiting as David cautiously approached the Roman soldier.

What do I say? David thought to himself as he neared the Roman. *Why am I even doing this?*

"Um, greetings," David said. The Roman was still gazing at the synagogue and did not appear to notice him. He cleared his throat and said it louder. "Greetings!"

The Roman jumped slightly and his eyes seemed unfocused when he turned to David, like he was still searching a point beyond him. "What is it?"

"I … can't help noticing, sir, that you seem to be looking for something. Perhaps I can help you?"

At this the Roman's eyes focused sharply on David. "What? Why?" He paused. "Why do you think you can help me?"

David stared at him, dumbfounded. He hadn't any idea how to answer the man. He did not even know this village; he was just passing through. How could he possibly help locate anything? "Ummm…"

The Roman grunted and strode away, leaving David feeling foolish in the middle of the avenue. Then the man turned slightly and glanced to the side, his back still toward David. "You don't know where I could find Yeshua of Nazareth, do you?"

David's mouth felt dry. He flushed, and was surprised at a sudden leap of excitement within him. He felt terrified – what if the Romans were out to arrest Yeshua? But this man was alone.

Why would he be looking for Yeshua to arrest him if he had no other soldiers to help him? Unless he was an advance scout and there were others waiting at a secondary location for him to report back. David almost said that he had no idea who the man was talking about.

But there was this strange sense of exhilaration rushing through David. For some reason he had this conviction that maybe he *could* help this man, Roman though he be. "Yes, I know where Yeshua is."

The Roman turned fully around to face David. He appeared suddenly unsure of himself. "You… you do?"

David nodded. "I am among those traveling with him. I can take you to him."

The Roman approached and, adjusting his tunic, cleared his throat and extended his hand. "Marcus, of the…" Instead of giving his rank and division within the Roman forces, the man shook his head. "I am Marcus."

David clasped his arm. "I am David."

Andrew came up behind David and nodded at Marcus, his arms full of goods. "My name is Andrew. Come with us and we will take you to Yeshua."

The three of them began walking, drawing many looks from incredulous, and sometimes angry, passersby. David noticed that the further they went the more on edge Marcus became. His hand kept straying to his sword hilt. This made David nervous, but Andrew seemed unconcerned.

"May we ask you, sir, why you are seeking Yeshua?"

David expected the Roman to say that Andrew should mind his own business, but instead he stopped in the middle of the road, and his eyes took on that faraway look from before. "I was guarding a man," he said. He slowly began walking again, and Andrew and David fell in step on either side of him. "I am one of the guards who watch over King Herod's prisoners. One day they brought in the wildest looking man I had ever seen. He had very long hair, was dressed in animal skins, and spoke in the strangest terms. They called him John the Baptizer."

David caught Andrew's glance. John was Yeshua's cousin and a prophet who had announced his coming.

"He was a special favorite of Herod's prisoners," Marcus went on, "in that he was treated both worse and better than the others, depending on the day and the whim of Herod. I was assigned to keep watch day and night on John, though he was not quarrelsome or likely to try escaping – anything but. This surprised me, for I had heard of this man. I heard that he preached scalding words against authorities both foreign and of his own people, loud and abrasive. I was expecting a fighter. I was therefore intrigued to see that he was very quiet most of the time. I am not in the habit of paying much attention to prisoners, but this one was so strange and obviously had the attention of Herod. So I watched him. The longer he stayed there, weeks and weeks, the darker his eyes became.

"His followers were able to squeeze in to see him every once in a while, and one day he, as agitated as I had seen him, asked them to find a man he called Yeshua and ask him if he was the one they had been waiting for, or if they should expect another."

Andrew nodded. "I remember when John's disciples came."

Marcus looked at him in surprise. "You were there?"

"Yes. I am one of Yeshua's disciples." He gestured at David. "He is, too."

Marcus paused, then shook himself and carried on. "I was rotated out briefly, and when I came back I could tell something was different with John. He was gazing up, and he sat still, sunlight hitting his face from the one gap high in the wall. I think that was the first time I had seen him turned toward the light. He looked peaceful, content even. I heard from the guard who had filled in for me that John's followers had come earlier that day and told John that 'the blind see, the lame walk, those with leprosy are cured, the deaf hear, the dead are raised to life, and good news is being preached to the poor.' My comrade had written down the words because of their strange power. He said that John had been as I then saw him ever since he had heard their words.

"It was not long after that we received word that John was to be executed. It fell to me to do the job, and…" Marcus trailed off.

Andrew had recoiled instinctively, and was looking down at Marcus's sheathed sword.

Calm beyond his understanding, David laid a hand on Marcus's shoulder. "Continue, friend."

Marcus glanced at him, then continued, looking at the ground as they walked. "…and when I took him outside to do what had to be done, I could not bring myself to raise the sword. John looked so *peaceful* still, as if… as if he had done everything he needed to do, and that this was simply his time to go. He looked as if nothing could possibly go wrong ever again. So I asked him. I said, 'John, aren't you afraid? Aren't you angry? Your life is about to be taken from you.' And you know what he said?"

"What?" David asked before he was aware he was speaking.

"He said, 'Marcus, you need to find Yeshua of Nazareth. He is the one we have been expecting. He is…' Here John paused, as if he were savoring the next words. He closed his eyes as he said, 'the Lamb of God who takes away the sins of the world.' "

David could see that Andrew was crying silently.

Marcus's eyes were misty. "And then I … beheaded him." He paused, as if considering for the first time the heaviness of what he had done. He glanced at Andrew, who was wiping his eyes, and then looked to David imploringly. "I'm so sorry. It was my job. But… It somewhat felt like it was the right moment. It was like he was ready, as if he had completion." Marcus rubbed his neck. "I've seen it so many times, death. In my work I have seen a lot of things. A lot of things. But I'd never seen someone face death so calmly, and so …'peacefully' is the word I keep coming back to. I want that peace. I face death every day, and it sometimes keeps me awake at nights. I need that peace. So the next chance I got, I set off to find this Yeshua of Nazareth. I have this impression…" He stopped walking. He was trembling, and David and Andrew stood with him. "I have this impression," he said, clearing his throat, "that I am on the edge of discovering something that will change my life. Part of me wants to stop before I get to that moment, to go back to what I already know. But I can't stop, I can't help it. I have to see this Yeshua for myself."

David and Andrew exchanged looks. Andrew pointed ahead of them. "You're right, friend. That house up ahead? Yeshua's inside it. Your life *is* about to change." Andrew motioned to David. "David, I think you should take Marcus inside."

David nodded at Marcus and began to walk forward, but the man stood still. He was looking at the house, but couldn't seem to make himself move. David placed a hand on his back and guided him forward. When they got to the door they heard the sound of talk and laughter from within. David placed his hand on the door and pushed.

The door swung open, revealing a long table, the disciples reclining around it. The patron must have been wealthy, because the board was full of good food, plenty for all. At the far corner, sitting in a pool of sunlight, was Yeshua. He stood up and smiled broadly. "Welcome, David! I saved you a seat next to me."

David smiled. "I think that seat is meant for someone else today." He drew Marcus in behind him and had him stand beside him. Several gasps arose from those gathered, and a woman who had been carrying plates to the table held them tightly to her chest. "A Roman!"

"Welcome, Marcus," Yeshua said, holding out his hands. "Come. There is a seat for you here."

Marcus was like one in a trance. Taking off his sword belt, he dropped it on the floor by the doorway and, hardly looking at where he was going, made his way around those on the ground until he stood before Yeshua in the sunlight. His hands were shaking, and without a word he knelt at Yeshua's feet. Yeshua smiled down at him, bent, and stood him up. He looked into Marcus's face, and the soldier wept. Yeshua pulled him to his chest in a strong warrior's embrace. When they parted Marcus was smiling, and they took their seats together.

The meal continued, and David and Andrew found seats among the others. They answered a few questions about why there was a Roman at the meal. Several people were angry, some were scared, but none made any trouble. David knew Yeshua would talk to them.

As he reached for the bread, David felt Yeshua's eyes on him. He looked up. Yeshua was talking with Marcus, but he glanced beyond Marcus for a moment and looked at David; his smile broadened as he kept speaking, and then his eyes were back on Marcus. David smiled to himself and tucked that moment away in a safe place in his heart as he continued eating. He felt Yeshua's pride in him, and knew then that they were partners, working together to draw others into the love of the Father. He wasn't next to Yeshua in that moment, but he never felt closer.

9

Beautiful Sorrow

It was a quiet evening, and David and Yeshua were spending time together, walking down a deserted path. Simon and the others were in town, enjoying some good food and fun after a gloriously rare and restful day.

David lived for these walks. Recently Yeshua had been asking him every few days to take a stroll, and he always gladly accepted the invitation. Sometimes they would get interrupted by someone approaching Yeshua asking for help, or one of the group coming to him to resolve a dispute or with a question, and their walk would be derailed. But Yeshua always made sure that there was a next walk. It seemed important to him, as if he had some specific purpose in mind. And yet each time it felt as natural as breathing, and things flowed so freely between them, that David resolved not to wonder and to simply delight in these times with his friend.

On these walks they sometimes talked, and sometimes they walked in silence, content with each other's company and the quiet sounds of the world around them. David was learning from Yeshua the value of quiet, and he no longer feared pauses in conversation. He was coming to appreciate stillness. In stillness, he became more aware of the Father, who, Yeshua said, was there, loving him, even though he couldn't sense him. He became more aware of Yeshua as well, this bright presence at his side.

Tonight they were talking. They discussed the day, and then went over how David had fared when he had recounted his experience of the little girl's resurrection. It had been with a group of young people who had listened eagerly to the tale. Yeshua had purposefully been standing a little distance away in another conversation, so that David could learn to share on his own with confidence, and so that those who listened would feel safe to encounter that moment of David's testimony themselves through his storytelling, without pressure of having Yeshua directly in their midst.

"You did very well," Yeshua said, smiling. "You nearly had me laughing in the middle of my own conversation, though – I kept feeling you staring a hole in my back."

"I was so nervous!" David chuckled. "You'd think I'd never told a story before in my life."

Yeshua put his hand on David's shoulder. "I know. But you needn't be nervous. You are a great storyteller." He smirked. "And that's coming from me – you see the crowds *my* stories draw."

"Yes, yes, you're pretty incredible, we get it." David shoved Yeshua lightly and they laughed.

"To be serious, though – I am so proud of you, David," Yeshua said. "You have grown so much."

David flushed with a pleasant mixture of pride and embarrassment.

"You are so open now," Yeshua continued, "where before you were closed off and aloof. See how well you get on with people you have just met. You laugh easily and freely. And you have learned to trust both me and others, where before you analyzed everything within an inch of its life. You are freer."

David nodded and sighed with contentment, pleased that he saw this progress in himself as well. "You know it's all due to you, Yeshua."

"Well, it's a partnership," Yeshua said. "You know I will not force change on you; you must always be willing—"

"Willing to start, yes." David smiled, and allowed himself a moment more to turn this idea over in his mind. He had started, hadn't he? He had let Yeshua in, had let him speak into his life. And he had seen changes in himself, glimpses of a new person he had never imagined he could be. He thought of Simon as he spoke at the inn, and he thought of Ari when Yeshua sent him out. Look who they had become. And he looked at himself. He thought back to who he had been when he first encountered Simon in the market, on that day that felt so long ago. He saw who he was now. He *had* started. He didn't know where it would lead him, but he knew, tonight, that something had assuredly changed. And he couldn't help wondering: where would it lead?

He shook himself. But there would be time for that later. "Speaking of starting, Yeshua, do you think we should start heading back?" He pointed and glanced back the way they had come. "It's getting dark, and our walk has taken us farther than usual."

"Friend…"

David turned back. Yeshua had stopped walking, and was turned toward him. He saw his friend's face, and his hand dropped to his side. That expression of both happiness and sadness was one David knew; he had seen it before. It startled him to see it now, but only for a moment. His heart tightened. Of course. Everything in the conversation tonight had been leading to this moment. He exhaled and his gaze flickered downward. "I see."

Yeshua walked over to him, a knowing smile on his face. "You know. It is time for you to take your own path."

David smiled sadly. "It just became clear."

Yeshua put his arm around David's shoulder. "But what a great way to end it – We laughed so much today!"

David's smile lost its sadness. "Yes, we did."

"You knew you would have to continue on in the world sooner or later."

Wiping at the corners of his eyes, David muttered, "Yes, but this is sooner."

"We have had weeks together, David, and in that time you have become so much more the man I know you can be – the man our Father and I designed, the one we created that clearing for."

David's lip trembled and his eyes misted at that memory – his first real talk with Yeshua. He hung his head, overcome with emotion.

Yeshua put his hands on David's shoulders. "In this time you have become so much more that man – the man we knew would minister to Rachel, would reach out to Marcus. You are sensitive to people's needs. You are meant to be a comforter, David, someone who reaches out with my love to those lost and confused. But your self-protective aloofness and overthinking were standing in the way. You needed to experience my love up close and know me. And look at you now!" There was a catch in his voice. "You now are able to connect with others. You prayed for that young man today! You would have never done that before. I am so proud of who you are becoming."

For a moment David's heart swelled, until the thought occurred to him – Did Yeshua do all this just to make him more usable for his purposes? David looked up and saw that tears were on Yeshua's cheeks. Immediately he remembered Yeshua's love for him. He opened his mouth to apologize for thinking that way, but he saw Yeshua mouth, "It's okay."

They embraced, then, a strong and trembling embrace. David felt the fierceness of Yeshua's love for him, and a new power of purpose surged through him. Moments throughout this journey flashed in his mind, moments of laughter, pain, revelation, and joy, moments that showed who he used to be and who he was becoming.

"Believe it," Yeshua whispered in his ear. "This is who you are."

This is who I am. That sentence turned from reflection to realization, and it ignited a strength and power that burned up from his heart into his limbs, and he squeezed Yeshua tightly. "You're right," he said. "This is who I am. Thank you, Yeshua, for everything. I love you."

"I love you, too."

They parted, and David smiled and wiped his eyes. "I am going to miss you."

Yeshua sniffed. "And I you. Remember always that you and I are bonded, friends closer than brothers. Our friendship is unique, and I will miss you greatly. But you are meant to touch the world, David. There is power in you; walk out your journey and release it into others in my name."

The wind picked up, whipping their clothing and hair, and David felt in it a pleasure and a presence. He stood taller. "Say goodbye to the others for me? Especially Simon?"

Yeshua nodded. "I will."

David smiled, lifted a hand in farewell, and turned toward the road.

"Oh, David, one last thing--"

David turned back, and barely had time to shout in surprise as Simon barreled into him. His field of vision filled with Simon's shirt as the big man scooped him up in a crushing hug, his booming laugh ringing out in the night.

"—Why don't you tell Simon yourself?" he heard Yeshua call with a chuckle.

"What?" David spluttered in shock and delight. "What are--" He broke off as Simon dropped him to his feet again and he staggered. He saw the other disciples coming to join them on the path, and he saw a fire flicker to life in the woods to one side. "What are you all doing here? I thought you were in town!"

"We were!" Andrew said, appearing beside him. He guided David to a seat by the fire and produced a caramelized date, David's favorite, and dropped it in his hand. "Buying supplies for tonight's festivities in your honor. Yeshua told us that today was the big day, that he was sending you out tonight. We couldn't just let you go without a celebration!"

"Celebration? For me?" David repeated, speaking around the bite of date in his mouth.

"Of course!" said a voice behind him.

David turned and craned his neck upward and saw John. The young man was grinning as he took a seat next to him. "How can we not celebrate? You came to us an observer--"

"A heckler!" Simon called, a playful growl in his voice. "Don't forget how he challenged Yeshua in front of the whole crowd that first morning!"

David blushed as everyone laughed. "How could I forget? I was so annoying!"

This elicited further laughter from the group, who were gathering around the fire with packs of food and skins of drink from the markets.

"Exactly!" John continued. "You came to us ready for debate, and you leave us as our brother. I personally think that transformation is worthy of rejoicing."

"Yes, and even more than that!" Phillip said. "When someone encounters Yeshua and his life is changed, he becomes a different person, worthy of rejoicing indeed. But then he goes into the world becoming the person he was always meant to be, to do what he was designed to do."

David glanced at Yeshua, who nodded, and he knew they both were recalling Yeshua's words after Ari left.

"And how much more we rejoice!" Phillip finished.

David looked around at these men, his friends, as they laughed and smiled at him. He saw their faces flickering in the firelight, and he realized how much he loved each of them. Tears wet his cheeks. "But… but isn't it hard?" he asked, a lump in his throat. "Saying goodbye?"

"Yes," Andrew said simply. "Yes, it is very hard. But I think," he said, pausing to gaze into the flames. "I think it is important that it is hard. Most worthwhile things are, you know. If it were easy then that might be cause for concern. The fact that it is hard means that you loved well."

Simon nodded. "Every time I leave my wife it is hard."

"But it is also so exciting," Andrew said, his eyes shining. "Because the one who is leaving knows he is following God's very design for his life, and that God will bring him fulfillment in every step of the journey, even when things are difficult, because it is his very own path that the Lord created for him by hand."

"Agreed. Your whole life," John said, "has been preparing you for this moment. Your entire stay with us was just a preparation for this next adventure, this great assignment, where you actually walk in your calling."

As those words hung in the air, David felt them inviting him to be of good cheer. He allowed the truth in them to penetrate his sadness at leaving these men and to change his perspective. He smiled, and felt that swelling pride and anticipation fill him again, that same iron conviction. *This is who I am.* He breathed in the wonder of discovering and walking in his purpose.

"And those who are left behind," Simon said, his voice thick, "are so proud of their friend who is setting out into his calling." He stared at David as if he might pierce him with his gaze, then wiped a hand across his eyes and took a huge bite into his bread.

They sat around the fire together, sharing the rich food and laughing, talking, and singing for several hours. At one point Yeshua had each of them share something they saw in David, and David wept openly, touched by their kindness and awed at the qualities they saw in him. With each person's words he was loaded with truth that grounded him and filled with hope that lifted him, as he received again and again the incredible conviction that God really was transforming him into a new man, into his true self.

When the time for departure had come, they presented him with provisions for several days and a new cloak, which Yeshua said he and John had picked. To David's continued surprise, it had a note from Rachel pinned to it, for it was from her that they had bought it. The note thanked him again and shared the news that her husband Levi was on the mend and doing better every day. The doctor had called it a miracle. David tucked the note in his pack for safekeeping.

After the final embraces with the disciples, Yeshua led David a short distance away. He smiled. "Are you ready?"

David closed his eyes. He wanted to fully take in this moment, to savor it, memorize it. He heard the muted talk of the disciples, felt Yeshua's strong hands on his shoulders. He felt the cool breeze playing with his hair, and unless he was mistaken, he thought he heard a faintly burbling stream somewhere in the distance. He smiled. It was time.

And with that realization, David felt the deep pang of a most beautiful sorrow, a kind previously unknown to him. It was all the heartache and sadness of an ending, intertwined indelibly with peace, joy, and the exhilaration of a monumental new beginning.

He opened his eyes. "Yes, I am ready, Yeshua."

Yeshua smiled broadly with pride. His hand tightened gently on David's arm. "This is not goodbye, you know. All roads lead to my father's house in the end for those who love me."

David nodded, smiling at Yeshua's blurry face through tears.

They embraced. Then David waved at everyone a final time, took a deep breath, and picked up his pack. He turned onto the road and strode out into the night.

The next morning when David woke, he expected to be surrounded by the disciples. In the bleary first thoughts of wakefulness, he glanced at the sun and wondered if he had slept late and missed breakfast. Then he remembered.

He got up to wash. As the water dripped from his face, he remembered how Yeshua had squeezed him tight in their final embrace. As he dressed, he remembered all Yeshua had said to him.

Now Yeshua was gone. There was just David and the dusty road ahead of him. Walking back to his camp, he glanced back the way he had come the previous night. Back that way were the disciples and Yeshua. He thought of their surprise goodbye feast, the stories, and the jokes. He thought of all they had said they saw in him. He then thought of Yeshua and the disciples preparing for a day full of ministry, and imagined being with them. He sighed. What had been so beautiful had ended. He looked forward, down the road he now must travel. He felt a twinge of apprehension. He was no longer feeling as confident as he had last night. He began to worry – what next? How would he communicate all he had seen? What would life look like for him now?

But he remembered what he had learned about the benefits of worry: there were none. David refocused his thoughts. He thought of Yeshua. He remembered all he had learned from him. He remembered the feeling of Yeshua's hand on his shoulder, his smile, his laugh. He recalled their talk in the clearing made for him the night David had put his faith in Yeshua. He remembered that Yeshua was much more than a man. And, glancing at the natural beauty of the morning around him, David remembered his own new connection to the Father, through the Son.

As he prepared a simple breakfast over a small fire, David turned over in his mind the importance of the truth that he had been sent out. This sending was like nothing he had experienced before in his life. So many times life had just seemed to happen, things falling into place one way or another without much direction. And he had been sent away before, away from community to do things on his own, alone. What happened last night was nothing like that. This sending was new, and it was right. His friends believed in him and were cheering him on. And Yeshua had entrusted something precious to him, an urgent message to any who would receive it. It was a message of hope and salvation, about knowing and being known by Yahweh, and about a friendship deeper than brotherhood. David felt a mounting excitement as he considered the places this road might lead, the hearts that might be turned toward Yeshua by his words and by how he lived. This was his calling, what he was created to do. He let himself dwell on that fact, let it grow larger and more and more real in his mind, until the overwhelming size and weight of it pushed him to his feet, overawed and a little dizzy with its power.

As he doused the fire, shouldered his satchel, and began to walk down the dusty road, he did not feel as alone as he had when he woke. In fact, David knew he would never be truly alone again. And he had the feeling that as he lived out his purpose, sharing Yeshua with others, companions would come alongside him, and that vibrant, deep community would grow where the name of Yeshua was elevated. He fixed his eyes on the horizon, said a prayer to his Father, and let the joy rise as he set out on his great assignment.